The First Line

An Anthology by the
Monash Writers Group

Tale

First Published 2018

National Library of Australia Cataloguing-in-Publication entry
Creator: Monash Writers Group, author.
Title: The First Line: Monash Writers Anthology.
ISBN: 978-0-6483273-3-2 (paperback)
Subjects: short stories.

Cover design by Cathy Larson.

Tale Publishing
Melbourne Victoria

Other Anthologies by

the Monash Writers Group

View from the Hill

Contents

Man's Best Friend by Bishnu Addison 3

An Unusual Point of View by Mube Akinci-Desem 16

The Type Writer by Sasha Buntman 25

Mystery Lights at Sea by Stephen Ellis 29

The Howling by Ingrid Fry 45

Where There's Life, There's Hope by Ingrid Fry 51

Same Thing, No Difference by Sakuntala Gananathan 56

Fortitude by Margaret Hepworth 63

What a Coincidence by Marlene Laurent 70

Kicking and Screaming to Heaven by Sung-Ju Suya Lee 81

A Reconciliation Myth by Bala Mudaly 94

The Coat Hanger by Robert New 104

Tangle by Andy Russell 118

A Portrayal of Defeat, and Hope by Robert Sayegh 126

Snakes Alive! by Brook Tayla 131

The Test by Erica Tippett 142

About the Authors 153

Introduction

Welcome to the Monash Writers Group's second anthology. After our first anthology, *View from the Hill*, people kept asking when we were going to release the next one. This started the ball rolling and at one of our meetings, we agreed to go ahead and produce a second collection. The theme for our first anthology was chosen due to the location we hold our meetings in—the Wheelers Hill Library—which is at the top of a hill and has wonderful mountain views. We wanted to keep with the idea of having a theme which was personal to us. To this end, after much brainstorming, we settled on the idea of taking the first line from a story we liked or were inspired by, and using it as the opening line of a new story. This way we could pay homage to the masters, learn about the power of an opening line, and also show our own literary preferences. We have a diverse membership and the opening lines range from classic literature to pulp fiction. Similarly, the genres our authors have written in range from historical fiction, science fiction, crime, mystery and even mild horror.

Any book like this requires the input of many people, so thanks to our editor, Kim Smith, for her elevating our work with her feedback on draft stories and proofreading the final manuscript. Thanks too, to our cover designer, Cathy Larson, who has made our book look amazing. Thanks also to the Monash City Libraries for sponsoring and promoting the Writers Group. The biggest thanks must go to the members of the Monash Writers Group for their hard work and dedication to the project. They spent nearly a year working on this from deciding on the theme to the launch of the book. Their patience, perseverance and entertaining stories have produced a collection which we hope you enjoy as much as we have putting it together.

Robert New
Chair, Monash Writers Group

Man's Best Friend

Bishnu Addison

A story has no beginning or end, arbitrarily one chooses that moment of experience from which to look back or from which to look ahead.[1]

'Come along Rover time for a walk, let's go before the joggers arrive and invade the park,' suggested Jack to his faithful companion. When they arrived at their destination, he let the dog off the lead, patted him fondly and saying, 'good boy, off you go and have a good run, but no chasing the birds or rabbits. I'll be right here on this old bench, stretching my arthritic limbs.' Jack

[1] First line from *The End of the Affair*, Grahame Greene

muttered while Rover bolted to enjoy his freedom. Being a childless widower, Jack turned to his four-legged friend for companionship. He had found the mongrel abandoned at a public carpark, shivering and whimpering, curled up into a tiny ball. He had put it in his car and taken it home, hoping Dot would let him keep it.

'Look, what I found Dot, isn't he cute?'

She cast a perfunctory glance at the wretched creature but was unmoved.

'You don't plan to keep it do you, Jack?' queried his wife.

Due to her unfortunate allergy to animal fur she had never had a pet in her life. Over the years she had developed a strong aversion to most animals, especially hairy ones.

'Give it away or take it to the RSPCA,' she ordered.

Jack was determined to keep this dear little puppy, so he decided to play a trick on his wife. He took the puppy out of the cardboard box and said, 'OK Dot, I have a painless solution'.

'What's that,' Dot asked with a glimmer of hope in her voice at the prospect of getting rid of the mongrel.

'I'll take it down to the creek and drown it.'

Dot's jaw dropped, her eyes blazed in disbelief and she shouted, 'Jack Miller, you murderous man, your cruelty knows no bound. Are you insane?'

'Rather than assign him to an uncertain miserable life, why not end it all in one go?' Jack asked, realising his trick might work. He had no intention of drowning the puppy, he was merely manipulating Dot to allow him to keep it. His bluff worked.

Dot agreed to let him keep the puppy provided it lived outside. The deal was done. It would be Jack's dog, but the rules were Dot's. The dog was not to set foot indoors, no chasing the chooks, no digging in the veggie patch. This was how Rover became a member of the Miller household.

A year later, Dot's health deteriorated. Her condition, exacerbated by her lifelong allergies, saw her succumb to emphysema. Her death brought Jack and Rover closer than before. Rover enjoyed the pampering and attention and most of all he enjoyed being indoors, especially on the cold winter days and nights. The twice a day walk was fun as well, he could run around frightening the birds and ducks on the pond. One could almost detect a mischievous grin on his face as he chased his avian enemies.

~

'Very refreshing running in the park, was it? Good to be back home in front of the fire though, isn't it?' Rover cocked his head, desperately trying to comprehend what Jack was saying. But his canine intelligence didn't stretch beyond basic commands. He went to lie down in his cozy basket to wait for some treat which always followed a run around in the park. Rover gobbled up his dog biscuit and began sniffing under the table, expecting to find more goodies.

It was a beautiful spring day, the birds were chirping

and fighting over the fat juicy worms. Suddenly the phone rang breaking the silence in the kitchen.

'Who could be ringing so early in the day,' he wondered as he picked up the phone, 'Hello Jack speaking. Oh, it's you, Jim, what news? I'm just sitting here enjoying my breakfast. I'm sorry to hear that, I didn't know he was sick. Oh, heart attack! Poor Des, he was a very decent old soul. I'll miss him. Yes, yes, I'll be there at the funeral on Saturday. Thank you for letting me know, Jim. See you at the church. Bye for now.'

~

The sudden passing of a friend shook him deeply. After breakfast, he picked up the paper and made a valiant effort to read, but the letters danced on the white background, mocking him. The bright morning sun made him drowsy and grumpy. 'Oh there's always bad news in the papers; war, death, destruction, I have a good mind to stop buying it, it's getting expensive too, can't afford to fritter away my meagre pension from Centrelink,' he said putting down the paper.

Jack often broke into a monologue, a habit he had developed after Dot died. With the passing of time, it was getting worse. He did it to show his discontentment or approval. Under the present circumstances, it was just for the ears of his canine friend who could not enter into a meaningful dialogue.

He then passed a cursory glance at his small living/dining area and kitchen and concluded it was satisfactorily tidy. He looked out into his backyard and realised both his window and veggie patch, needed cleaning and tidying up.

Rising slowly, he steadied himself holding on to his chair and stood there as if in a trance. Then he called out to his friend again, 'come on Rover, let's go and work in the garden before the weeds choke my beans and tomatoes. But remember the orders Ma Dot left you. No digging in the garden to bury bones, if you do, you will be banned from the veggie patch.' Although he was an intelligent dog, Rover's sense of right and wrong was limited. He didn't understand the warning given. So he just wagged his tail and happily followed Jack into the veggie garden wondering where he had buried his last shank bone.

The grandfather clock in the hall struck twelve heralding the time for lunch. On the last stroke, Jack put his gardening tools down and went inside, followed by Rover wagging his tail. There was a great expectation and joy on his face knowing Jack had come in to prepare lunch. Another pot of tea and some wholemeal sandwiches and dry food for his dog. Jack sat in his favourite wicker chair munching his sandwich lost in reverie.

~

He thought Des was a lucky man, he hadn't had to spend time in a nursing home. 'That's the way I want to go,' he said aloud and woke his dog who looked at him with soulful eyes. He knew his friend was hurting, he had that *how can I help you* look on his face, but couldn't utter his concern. He just put his head on his paws and whimpered.

These days Jack spent his time reminiscing and worrying about his own, and Rover's, future. 'Who will take this aging mutt?' he asked himself, but got no answer. Time dragged on as it has the habit of doing when one is old and lonely. Des' funeral was a very sombre event. There were only a handful of people attending, his widow and a few geriatric friends including himself. All stooped with age, they watched the coffin retreat behind the curtain while *Amazing Grace* played softly in the background. The gray-haired widow wiped tears from her eyes as the music stopped and the coffin disappeared. The minister announced, 'please stay for some refreshments the church members have laid out in the hall'.

One of the ladies handed Jack a cup up tea which he thankfully received. 'Thank you, I'm parched this is exactly what I needed, a strong cup of tea to warm me and of course, the sponge and slices look divine too.' They all huddled around with cups of tea, munching the cakes and biscuits but deep in thought. They were all reflecting on Des' passing which brought home their own mortality.

'See you all, keep well,' he said to the widow and left the hall to get home and feed Rover. When he arrived home the pooch wasn't there. He didn't come to greet him as was his customary practice, expecting a pat and some delectable reward for guarding the house. He opened every door including the back door and looked but there was no Rover. Panic-stricken he called out, 'here boy, walkies, come on, let's go to the park and chase the birds'. Still no sign of Rover. Jack went in and sat down and debated. 'Should I call the police or any of the neighbours?' he asked himself as he sat there, unable to take any action until he heard a yelp from over the fence. Buoyed by the hope of finding his dog, he tiptoed to the fence and spotted Rover frolicking with another dog—biting each other's ears and tails and provoking each other—lost in a playful, friendly fight. Mixed emotions overwhelmed him. He was relieved that no harm had come to his four-legged friend. But he was consumed by jealousy that his canine companion of many years had found a mate from his own species—discarding him without a second thought. He felt dejected and alone; he longed for Dot. He felt betrayed and abandoned by his trusted friend. He was deeply wounded.

He tried to shake himself out of his self-pity. He admonished himself sharply, 'grow up Jack, it's only a dog. Human friends sometimes find a new friend and abandon the old one, it's the way of the world. Get on with your life. Dot would laugh at your naivety. Oh, I know I'm a senile old fool. I ought to be ashamed of myself.' It was getting dark and chilly, so he switched on the light and reluctantly entered the kitchen in search of something to eat. Suddenly he realised he was starving. Of course, his daily routine was to feed Rover first, only then he would prepare his own meal.

~

He filled Rover's bowl with food and placed it on the laundry floor and called out, 'here boy, din-din' and waited, wondering whether his friend would respond. Surprisingly he came in panting, followed by his new-found friend. Together they gobbled up the food and went to the backyard to frolic over his precious veggie patch. 'Dot would be mortified,' he thought.

Jack was saddened by this change in his dog. The devoted lovable animal had turned into a rough street hound.

The following morning, he picked up the lead and whistled for Rover calling out, 'walkies, here boy park time,' no response. He peered into his kennel, but the mutt was gone. He put the lead back on the hook, poured himself a mug of tea from the teapot which was still warm, and flopped on the wicker chair to plan what action to take. The strong bond no longer existed, his dog did not lie at his feet providing him unconditional love and companionship. The occasional walk to the park was accompanied by the other dog. They no longer had any conversation because Rover was busy playing with the other dog and ignored him.

Jack's loneliness and boredom made him listless his desire to live was fading rapidly. One day his close friend Jim encouraged him to see his GP and get some medication. Out of respect for Jim, he went to see his GP. Surprisingly the wait wasn't too long. His name was called out, 'Mr. Miller'. He stood up painfully, leaning on his special four-pronged disability aid.

His GP stood at the consulting room door to receive him.

'Good morning Jack, come in, what can I do for you today?'

Greetings over, Jack sat down on the chair facing the doctor and explained the reason for his visit.

'I am always tired doctor, I have no appetite either.'

'Your dog must be tiring you, Jack. Don't take him for a walk twice a day. One walk daily should be sufficient.'

'I'll take your blood pressure too while you are here. Hmm, blood pressure is good for your age. You look all right to me, but I'll give a mild antidepressant that should help you to sleep better. Go out and see friends or work colleagues, you can't live in isolation like a hermit.'

'I have no close friend, I had a dog which was my closest companion. I didn't need anyone else.'

The doctor pounced on his comment, 'you said *had* does that mean you no longer have him?'

'No, no he's still with me physically but has found another four-legged friend from next door so he prefers to socialise with his own kind rather than with a geriatric human.'

The doctor laughed and said, 'nothing new there, Jack it happens with humans too. Our interests and needs change over time and we move on. You have to let go and turn to other interests. Join a club, find a new hobby.' After offering this platitude, he handed the prescription and gently touched his arm in a farewell gesture and walked out with him suggesting, 'come and see me in a fortnight to see if the tablets are helping.'

~

The pharmacist handed him the medication and explained, 'these tablets are to be taken daily preferably with your evening meal, so you get a good night's sleep.'

Jack nodded his head and put the medication in his pocket and shuffled out of the chemist.

He got home and unlocked the door expecting Rover to come bounding down the hallway, barking and wagging his tail to welcome him. But that was in the past now, he was too busy elsewhere having fun. He felt extremely fatigued, all he wanted to do was to sit on his wicker chair and think of Dot. Soon he dropped off to sleep due to sheer mental and emotional exhaustion. But was woken up by something nudging and licking his hand, which felt sticky and wet. He opened his eyes and saw that the house was plunged into darkness. He couldn't see anything until he got up and switched on the kitchen light. He looked around and saw Rover sitting beside his chair. 'Oh, it's you, found your way home, have you?' he said sarcastically. Rover just licked his hand and moaned softly.

'Missing your dinner, I suppose, come along then I'll feed you first.' Rover panted with excitement and ran around salivating. It was like old times again. Jack filled the bowl with a generous amount of food and placed it on the floor near the bowl of fresh water. The dog was ravenous, he devoured a mound of food in a twinkle of the eye. Jack instinctively patted him and said, 'all gone,' while Rover looked up expecting more. But when Jack went to his kitchen Rover knew there was no more food coming, so he quietly went to lie down in his basket in the laundry. He gazed at Jack pottering around in his kitchen, preparing his evening meal which consisted of steamed vegetables and lamb chops. He finally sat down to eat but had no appetite. He looked at the dog and recalled the day he had brought him home and how he had tricked his unsuspecting wife into letting him keep the miserable mutt. He said, 'now he is strong and healthy and he doesn't need me anymore'.

He pondered, if Dot were alive she would gently remind him, 'I told you not to keep that dog, now it's turned out to be an utter disappointment. However, don't brood, get on with your life.'

He pushed his plate away and stood up. 'Here boy you might as well enjoy my food as well, I'm not hungry but let me put it in your bowl.' Rover consumed the food and went back to his basket to chew the bones while Jack made himself a strong cup of tea and washed down the antidepressant tablet. He then dragged his chair closer to the open fireplace, draped his granny patchwork blanket over his knees, picked up Mitch Albom's *Tuesday with Morrie* and started reading it for the umpteenth time. The warmth of the fire and silence of the night lulled him to sleep. The book slid from his bony fingers and landed on the floor with a thud. Rover awoke and looked up. He saw the granny rug had caught fire, it was billowing thick smoke while Jack slept soundly. Rover jumped out of his basket and tugged at the rug and barked and growled as never before, but he could not wake Jack. He raced out barking and howling, by then the fire alarm was trigged, but the weatherboard home was engulfed in flame. Neighbours came to help but there was nothing they could do except ring the emergency services and wait. But Rover ignored the roaring fire, ran into the house disregarding the bystanders' warning, 'stay Rover. No!'

~

The neighbours were certain both Jack and his dog had perished in the blaze. But they witnessed a miracle. Someone shouted, 'look that crazy mongrel is dragging Jack by the ankle'. They all applauded, 'good dog, well done'. Jack had inhaled a lot of smoke but was still alive.

~

The fire brigade arrived but the old house was burnt to the ground. Fortunately, Jack and the dog were alive, paramedics lifted him onto the stretcher to take him to the hospital. However, Rover wouldn't let go, he howled, snarled and exposed his sharp canine teeth to stop them. Jack opened his eyes and patted his dog saying, 'good boy Rover, I'll be back soon,' and with those words he and the dog knew that all was forgiven, with no more animosity on either side. Rover continued to whine and upset Jack, so a kind bystander said, 'don't worry mate, I'll bring Rover to the hospital,' and patted the dog to pacify him. Finally, the ambulance left and Rover followed. The ordeal was over, everything was forgiven and forgotten. Jack lost his home but found his best friend, all was well with their world.

An Unusual Point of View

Mube Akinci-Desem

My working life has been a series of sideways slides, of adaptations rather than ambitions.[2]

At lunchtime...

In my humble view, life is more like a series of slides, some with faster action than others. Adapting is the name of the game here. If you haven't got the guts to fit in, then you are history.

Licking all my mouthparts, I note it's a sunny day

[2] First line from *True Stories*, Helen Garner

today. It's too bright for my liking. I need to keep myself clean. What's the saying, cleanliness is next to godliness? It must be true. If you keep yourself clean then you can enjoy life in a better state. Lunch was good. Yes, it was. I must say I'm still good at getting my own lunch.

I wonder what's out there tonight. I know what will happen if I continue to sit here; I will gradually fall apart and rot. I mean rot! I feel I need some excitement. At my advanced age one doesn't really care about the risks of everyday life, you know, the nitty gritty accidents and pushovers. The kind of stuff that will limit the adventures of weaker souls. Having lived this long I believe I have some old tricks up my sleeve.

This ancient body of mine is really slow these days. My stiff neck prevents me from seeing much further than the front lawn. My full abdomen doesn't encourage me to move fast either. I feel like going into a hole and hiding for a little while. I feel so sleepy. I think I will lie down and rest a little.

A few hours later...

Well, I feel so much better now. Sleep is the essence of life. It helps exude confidence for the shy and the weak-hearted. Now, I feel ready for the tough world outside. Having finally digested my lunch, I am, right now, rather more athletic than usual. Ha, ha, ha.

It's getting dark outside. Maybe, it's time I tour the main street and see what's cooking out there in this wide cut-blade world of ours. And give these old legs some exercise too.

Now. Look at this. It's a busy thoroughfare. There are creatures of all kinds out there. They all look ugly and mean. Everyone's out for themselves. I admit, these days I don't feel easy in the company of such cut-throat regulars. In my younger days, I used to roam the world like any bold roughie. I've had my share of blizzard attacks; the surprise invasions, and other pack drives of which I don't particularly wish to remember the gory details. No. I do not wish to remember the exploits and the ravages of time.

Hey! Ancient creature. Come back to the present before you are swallowed up out of existence in this damnable crawling thoroughfare.

OK. It smells fresh outside. Rather excitable. The wind is coming from the west. I can actually smell the desert. Let's get a move on, old man! I am not going all the way to the confines of the desert to find excitement. It's too far and dangerous to contemplate a trip out there. What's happening locally? Let's find out for ourselves.

Mmmm. Now, I like the smell of irresistible delicacies coming from inside this house. It is, however, too much of an effort to make it over the enormously high fences. I simply give up.

Now, this house on the left has no fences or gates. It should be easy to get close and find out what the occupants have been up to recently. It's very quiet on all fronts. Let's give it a try. I think I can attempt to move in from the laundry door. Hey! Now, I'm so lucky. They haven't secured the door, just as I expected.

Here we are. With a little effort, I am inside. It's awfully quiet. I don't have to hurry up. I have all night. I can just take my time and follow the smell. Mmmm. It's on the left. I'm in an alien environment. Let's do a thorough clean up first. I feel better already. My, my! This is a big house by any standards. How long will I walk to get to the end of this corridor? Well, I'll try my best.

I should first of all try to see what's in this room on the right. Wow! Lots and lots of books, books everywhere. These people must like books, to read them I mean. If you ask me there is nothing to find on all those pages with black squiggles. It would indeed be very boring to sit with a book in front of you for hours and hours. The story goes that there are some people, the very dedicated ones indeed, who have read all of these books, the books around me here, and more. I don't understand any of this, but, everyone to their own way.

This room has magical smells. Now, if I push my head in through the doorway I sense something extraordinary in this room. I can tell it straight away. When I pull my head back to the corridor, the sensation disappears—it's definitely in this room. It looks like I'm going to have to climb some of these timber decks that are lined up in all different directions, to get to the upper shelves. My sensory organs are tickled pink at the prospect of this extraordinary sensation. I am so excited. I've got to get to it. Now!

Up one. Down another. Up one, down another. Sideways and up again. Yes. This is how I have to spend my precious time tonight. This merry-go-round continues for so long, I am seriously about to give it up when the titillating sensation goes up a notch. Oh, my Creator! I just know when I get to the source of this amazing sensation I am going to be *so* rewarded. I feel dizzy with great expectation. Hang on! I shouldn't make any unnecessary noise. I don't want the whole household after me.

After several hours...

Oh, I think I just spotted it. I must be very close to it now. The beautiful sensation is unimaginably hair-tingling. Guess what! I certainly want to get high and lose myself in the joy of this mysterious feeling. The electrifying power of the century! Sshh. Don't scream now. When you are so close to it, don't go and ruin your chance of enjoying the ultimate experience, old one.

Here it is! I am coming. I found it. I found it. Wait for me! This excitement is too much for me. My heart is about to stop. These old legs of mine can't inspire me to move any faster. Dribbling all over doesn't help either. I need to clean myself. Cleanliness is next to godliness. I can't function if I am not clean. Grooming is the most important behaviour for a socially minded creature. One can breathe easier when one has thoroughly cleaned oneself.

I hope nobody else followed me into this house. I certainly don't want to share these titillating sensations with any stranger. At my age, I cannot fight and win to live another day against a member of the younger generation. I would die without the ultimate experience. It would be a pity. I don't want that. No! I definitely do not want that.

Now, let's see. I think the gorgeous smell is coming from the other side of that long thick book. If I can only see the other side. Unfortunately, I am not strong enough to push the book over. There are no spaces between the books; how perfectly they must have set them side by side. Admirable, if I was interested in books in any way. Now, what do I do? After coming all this way up, I can't possibly quit, can I? No! That's not in my nature. There must be a way to reach the other side of that ugly, fat book.

Yes. I will find a way. What's the saying, where there is a will, there is a way. Now, that's the spirit. Oh, I am trembling with great expectations. Little by little I push the book that looks big, I keep pushing. I keep pushing for minute after minute. I keep pushing. I push the fat book and I push the fat book. I have nothing to lose. I keep pushing. Every little bit helps. I keep pushing. I will keep pushing till my last breath. I keep pushing. I have nothing to lose, I might as well push. I keep pushing. Every little bit helps, I just keep pushing.

Sometime later…

There! I have access to the other side of the fat book. I moved the book a fraction. The sheer power of persistence. I can see. That's where the titillating sensation has been coming from all along. It doesn't look much like anything, but the smell is overpowering my senses.

Here we are. This book is open. It is full of pictures stuck together. Pictures of I don't care what. I can just put my tired head on these pictures and let go. My tired heart is going to stop. Too much excitement. Oh, it's a bit too much for me. I am in heaven. I … am … in … heaven. I … am … in … heaven. I … am … in … he … a … v … en.

In the morning…

I am suddenly woken up by this rude person who is screaming at the top of her voice. Strangely, she is screaming right next to me.

'Oh my God! Mum! Look at this!'

I slept so well. Who is this rude person waking me up with such a loud scream?

'Mum! There is a cockroach here! It's sitting on my scrapbook! What do I do?'

Shut up, rude person. Can't you be quiet? I've had a drunken night. Can't you see?

'Mum! It's sitting on my beautiful pictures! I think it's

stuck on the glue!'

Oh shush, rude person. You are killing me with your voice. Enough screaming, please.

'Mum! What do I do?'

Shut up. You are disturbing my sleep.

'OK, filthy creature! I'll show you.'

The rude person goes out and returns a little while later, her hands are now shiny and slippery.

'I will show you what it means to come into my study. You dirty cockroach!'

The rude person attempts to manhandle me.

'Mum! It's stuck on to my scrapbook. How do I get it off without squashing it?'

Oh, it hurts. The rude person is hurting me.

The rude person pulls me free of the picture book with some force and walks fast out of the room carrying me in her shiny hand.

'How dare you walk all over my scrapbook?'

Where are you taking me, rude person?

The rude person opens the laundry door and hurls me out over the fence.

Whoop, whoop, thrum! I hit a tree trunk and roll down to the ground.

Oh, it hurts. The rude person just threw me out like a piece of garbage. Was I inside her house? I must have fallen asleep on the heavenly picture book. I think I spent a long time looking for the picture book with the heavenly smell last night.

The rude person touched me everywhere. Yuck. How

disgusting! I feel so dirty. Quickly, I need to clean myself. I can't stand the alien smells. With some effort I dust myself. After I give myself a thorough clean, I straighten up and here I am. Never mind. I am still in one piece.

I guess it takes a lot of extra energy to crush this old body of mine. I feel invincible. I told you I have some tricks up my sleeve. Escaping alive from the hands of a human is the biggest win of the lottery today.

Ha, ha, ha. Boy! Did I have fun last night!

The Type Writer

Sasha Buntman

If you want to find Cherry-Tree Lane, all you have to do is ask the Policeman at the cross-roads.[3] And it was at number 7 Cherry-Tree Lane that the writer resided. The decadent little Edwardian cottage, with no other inhabitants.

The writer's daydream started to merge with reality, intersecting between his mundane, daily routine. At his desk, he attempted to twitch his shoulders and neck, to try to remove himself from the daydream. Fidgeting with his pen and nib, like a teenager sitting a test.

---

[3] First line from *Mary Poppins,* P. L. Travers

He discovered that he adored the blank piece of paper. Its infinite, intricate possibilities were implied–nestled and enveloped within its nothingness. He caressed its sleek, thin edging with optimism. He relished its crispness, the fresh feeling of the blank piece of paper. *This could be anything; this could be nothing*, he pondered while staring out the window. The vastness of the sky swallowed his daydream for ten minutes.

The writer's thoughts began unfolding, as though he was unwrapping a new gift. *Empty or full; meaningful or dull. It's whatever I make of it. I am in control, I hold the pen of personal power and can transform this blank page into a creation of my own imagination.*

A mass of blank white pages sits on the table—waiting anxiously to be filled, to be utilised. To be nourished with words and ink. He prefers these to notebooks or diaries because they can be discarded and then something new can be created. Whereas a journal is rather restrictive. Each page is expected to—indeed encouraged, to relate to one another. The writer fears he may make mistakes and then have to tear out a page or two. This is not the case with a piece of paper. It gives him permission to make mistakes, or to throw it out and start anew with another plain piece. It doesn't constrict his thoughts either or beg to belong to other sections of prose. It invites him to open up to its endlessness. A sense that there is no beginning or end. It's a snapshot, waiting to be taken. A slice of life and humanity, waiting to be shared.

The shiny, metallic pen sat tightly between the writer's fingers. Suddenly, it began to magically move across the paper in front of him. Words spilled out of it uncontrollably. His wrist shook vigorously, his heart pulsated and vibrated anxiously. *What's happening? It's doing it all by itself!*

After several minutes of non-stop writing, the pen's nib bounced off his hand and landed in the wastebasket—as if to imply 'I've given you a head start. Now it's your turn…' He read the page and held his chest in shock. He liked what he read.

Feeling inspired, the writer fished the pen from the wastebasket and began to write vigorously. Many hours dissolve away. Hundreds of pages are lumped together chaotically on the desk. They aren't blank anymore. Their energy seems to vibrate in the grotty room.

The writer manages to nervously approach the vintage typewriter, for the first time in over a year. The same typewriter that had contributed to the writer's current state of insanity. *Was it my craziness that caused me to become fearful of my typewriter? Or was it my typewriter that unravelled the moment when I knew I had completely lost my mind? I suppose I'll never know for sure.*

Not today. Today, the dusty typewriter was radiating with magical purpose and charm. Its punchy noises of triumph were spurring the writer on. His fingers typed automatically, as though on an urgent mission, flowing like a pianist sprinkled with stardust. Even the liquid in the cold cup of tea, sitting on the antique desk, jittered from the ecstatic speed of his typing.

Within the next 24 hours, the first draft of his novel was complete.

Mystery Lights at Sea

Stephen Ellis

Five minutes to three in the afternoon.[4] Daks, Willy, Kate, Sharon and Ted gather alongside Snake Creek, under the shade of a weeping willow. Yoko is missing. Sharon dips her toes into the cool shallow water.

'Watch out, Shaz,' Ted calls. 'Eels will bite ya!' Sharon scurries from the water's edge and joins her Tea Tree Bay Primary School friends.

'Glad school's out this arvo,' Kate smiles, 'to fix the electricity fault.'

'Yeah. But, it's too cold to swim,' Sharon grumbles,

---

[4] First line from *61 Hours*, Lee Child

as she puts on her shoes.

'Come on.' Willy directs the posse. 'Make a circle.' He sits with them and plonks the Friday morning Surf Coast newsletter of 19 October 1956 onto the grassy bank. He points to the headline: *Strange Lights at The Crags*. 'There, we need another tricky case to solve.'

'Yeah,' Daks agrees, rubbing the rabbit-trap scar on the back of his leg.

Ted jumps up. 'Well, we did solve who stole Mrs Nutmeg's eggs.'

'It wasn't *who*,' Kate interrupts, adjusting her sunhat. 'It was those cunning foxes.'

'Whatever.' Ted points at the sky. 'Them lights, could've been a flying-saucer.'

'Been reading your outer-space comics, again?' Sharon teases.

'My dad reckons,' Daks says, 'just dills fishin' at The Crags.'

Willy grabs the newsletter, stands up and shouts, 'Club Ozity detectives, we'll investigate and check things out tonight!'

'So much fun,' Sharon and Kate chorus.

Kate pretends to write with her finger. 'I can make lots of logbook notes.'

'All agree. Good.' Willy assumes. 'Okay, we'll meet up tonight at the quarry entrance. Daks can pick up Yoko on the way.'

Jeff likes his corny nickname, Daks, given to him by his new fourth-grade friends. Sharon taps Willy's arm.

'Yoko's still doing chores at the grocery store.'

'I forgot,' Willy groans. 'Can anyone leave a secret message under Yoko's little cactus pot plant?'

'Rightio,' Kate offers. 'Yikes, Yoko's big sister tells on her when she does stuff.'

'Yoko's lucky, she's got her own bedroom,' Sharon says. 'She can sneak out for sure.'

'What about you, Shaz?' Kate asks. 'Can you get away okay from your caravan?'

'Hope I can creep out after dark,' Sharon replies, biting her lower lip.

'My mum and dad go square-dancing on Friday nights.' Daks frowns. 'They'll come home late, find me out. They'll ground me.'

'Worrywart,' Ted says. 'We *all* want to go.'

Daks looks down while ruffling his hair.

Willy concludes, 'Ted, bring your dad's racing bin'ocs.'

~

Daks sits with his parents at the kitchen table, awaiting his favourite Friday night dessert. Mum asks, 'What are you doing tonight, Jeffrey?'

'Reading some comics I swapped with Willy. Wish we had a tel-lee-vee-sion, Dad.'

Dad looks at the ceiling for inspiration. 'Uncle Bert's got one of them new TVs son. We're planning to visit your Melbourne cousins. And, take you to the Olympic Games next month.'

'Wow! Great, Dad,' Daks mumbles, enjoying a

mouthful of homemade vanilla ice-cream sprinkled with hundreds and thousands. 'I'll take my autograph book. Mum can bring her camera.'

Mum smiles, looks at Dad. 'The church ladies are discussing the lights seen at The Crags. You hear any scuttle-butt?'

Dad shakes his head. 'Just the usual nonsense.' He leans forward on his elbows. 'Likely be car lights reflecting off the sea mist.'

Mum tilts her head. 'There's only a goat track up to the lookout.'

'Just saying what Friday's pub regulars reckon.' Dad sighs. 'Anyway, papers will print any old hogwash.'

'Maybe so, Henry. But, others across the inlet also saw strange lights, some blinking like a lighthouse.'

Daks's dessert bowl is empty, he looks up. 'Could've been rabbitos out spotlighting, or one of them fancy yachts we see at Christmas time?'

Dad blurts out, 'No skipper worth his salt will go near The Crags, son. The reef's far too dangerous at night.'

'But, I've seen 'em trawlers sink craypots along the rocky shoreline.'

'Not at night time, Jeffrey.' Mum clears the table. 'It's not called the *ship-wreck coast* for nothing.'

'A real big mystery, Mum.' Daks smiles. 'Any more ice-cream?'

~

After dark, the Club Ozity detectives finish packing their knapsacks in secret. Sharon takes her favourite black polka-dot pyjamas to sleepover over at Kate's place for the weekend. Sharon asks, 'What did you pack?'

'Some adventure things, Shaz,' Kate tells her. 'My torch, compass, matches, towel, logbook, pencil, water bottle, spare jumper and some sandwiches.'

'Wow. I got my pocket knife, yo-yo, and comics.' Sharon peeks at the full moon through Kate's bedroom lace curtains.

~

Later that evening, the children begin to tiptoe from their comfy bedrooms. Clouds scud past a bright moon. Kate and Sharon walk along a familiar narrow gravel track.

'I can hear the boys up ahead,' Kate says.

Ted bumps into Willy. 'Watch it,' Willy warns. 'Got ya dad's bin-ocs?'

Ted taps his knapsack. Kate and Sharon appear from the gloom. An owl hoots and swoops close past them. 'Jeepers,' Sharon cries.

'What kept ya's?' Ted says. 'Where's the other two?'

Kate checks who's missing. 'Can't be far away.'

Willy asks Kate, 'Did ya leave Yoko a message?'

'Sure did.'

More owl hoots. Sharon screws up her eyes.

After hanging about for fifteen minutes, Ted suggests, 'Let's go on without 'em.'

Willy strides towards the winding uphill track, looks back. 'Come on then, follow me.'

They trudge onwards into the darkness. Soon Sharon stops, hands on hips. 'We nearly there, yet?'

'Must be close,' Ted says. 'Can't ya hear the surf?'

'Push on,' Kate says, pulling down on her woollen-knitted beanie. She covers her nose. 'Yuk, rotting seaweed stinks.'

'Hooray,' Sharon cries, as they arrive at The Crags lookout.

'Dump ya bags.' Willy points to a patch of twisted tea tree. 'Let's set-up our spy camp.'

Sharon quivers. 'Glad there's no more owls out here.'

'Nah, just great big octopuses to get ya,' Ted jests. Sharon glares at him.

Kate checks the logbook roster she recorded in a blue-lined exercise book. 'Ted. Tonight, you're our first lead spy.'

'Thanks.' Ted adjusts his dad's binoculars, scans the churning sea.

'What's that behind us?' Willy is distracted, as a beam of light moves shakily along the pathway. Daks and Yoko wander sheepishly into the hideout.

'Sorry, we're so late,' Daks says, ruffling his hair. 'I fell asleep. Lucky for me, Yoko tapped on my window.' He drops their knapsacks onto the ground.

Big Willy looks at little Yoko. 'What's dat ya holding?'

'My picnic blanket and a map.'

'What map?' Willy snaps.

'Got us a local tourist map to mark crosses and compass bearings. You know, if we see anything. That's what good detectives do.'

Willy rolls his eyes and sighs. Cross-legged, they

huddle together on the blanket. Yoko fiddles with the map. Sharon takes a turn with the binoculars. Straightaway, she cries out, 'Look, there's a light!' Six pairs of eager eyes stare out to sea.

'I see it,' Willy says. 'Crikey, there's more of 'em.'

'Lots,' Ted says.

Daks, still embarrassed by sleeping in, asks Yoko, 'You're a clever sea scout, is it Morse code?'

'Nup. Just lights bobbing about on the waves.'

'Must be fishing boats?' Ted says.

'Check your compass.' Yoko bosses Kate. 'Record the bearing in the logbook.'

'Yep,' Kate replies.

Daks asks, 'Anyone got a watch?'

'I borrowed my sister's,' Yoko says. She flicks her torch on, checks her Koala-wristwatch. 'It's twenty past midnight. Note the time down, Kate.'

'There's a green light,' Ted points. 'Oh no, I don't see it anymore. It's all gone dark, again.'

'Anyone see lights?' Willy asks. A long silence, as no one replies.

Ted and Sharon begin to discuss *Phantom* comics, and share some lollies. Kate hands out peanut butter sandwiches. Another hour passes. Yoko yawns. 'I want to go home now.'

They agree to pack up camp and return to the comfort of their warm beds.

~

The Club Ozity members, sleepy-eyed and anxious, meet

at their school's shelter shed at midday on Saturday.

'What ya's reckon about last night?' Willy asks, straddling his bike.

'No news on the radio,' Daks says. 'Nothing in the morning paper about any more lights at sea.'

Kate clutches the logbook. 'How come no one else saw anything?'

'It was really late,' Ted shrugs.

'We had the best lookout,' Sharon boasts. 'So much fun.'

'Wonder what the green light meant?' Kate asks.

'Likely a signal to someone,' Yoko says. 'We must continue to spy.'

'Alright,' Willy agrees. 'We'll check out the beach this arvo. Who's coming?' Ted and Daks raise their arms.

'We've got netball practice at three o'clock with Miss Cutty at school,' Kate announces.

'We can scout the beach and report back,' Willy says.

'Great,' Ted says, 'I can do some tracking stuff my Grandpa taught me at Ayers Rock last Christmas.' They scatter on their bikes.

~

Five minutes past three in the afternoon. Willy, Ted and Daks wander in a single file along the sandy shoreline towards the headland. It's low tide. Seabirds scamper about looking for a feed of crabs. Daks enjoys the ebbing wash of water over his bare feet.

Willy and Ted, accustomed to Daks's dawdling, move across to the dunes. They push past salt bushes and sneak along an overgrown pathway. Ted trips over. 'Ouch!' He inspects his toes.

'Ups-a-daisy,' Willy calls. 'You okay?'

'Yep.' Ted crawls about and scrapes his hands in the sand. 'What's this?' He uncovers a hidden rope, leading to a clump of low foliage.

Daks catches up to them. They remove cut branches to uncover an inflatable dinghy and peek inside. Ted cries, 'Looks awful scary.'

'Careful,' Willy warns. 'Don't touch it. Stay back, Daks.'

Daks ignores him as he moves closer for a squiz. 'We must tell the police.'

~

Five minutes past four in the afternoon. The three boys dash along the beach, past the car park, past dog walkers, past the boat ramp. There are no telephone boxes near the foreshore. They turn inland towards town, sprinting to the police station. Willy leads the way with Ted in hot pursuit. Daks lags behind, hindered by his gammy leg.

Ted puts in a spurt of energy. He and Willy burst into the police station. Sergeant Hopkins sits behind a high counter. Startled, he spills his freshly brewed coffee when Willy and Ted scream, 'There's a dead man on the beach!'

~

Sergeant Hopkins inspects the dingy and pulls aside a crumpled tarpaulin. 'I see why you boys got such a big fright. Those yellow gumboots sticking out do look like legs. The tarp was covering scuba tanks and a roll of some kind of mesh-bags. The buoy looks like a head in this dappled light.' He motions the boys to come forward. 'Good on you for reporting this. The concealed dingy is suspicious.'

'Sorry, Sergeant,' Daks offers. 'We really thought...'

'No worries, young fella. You've never seen a *real* dead body before. We'll all go back to the station. I'll phone your parents.'

~

At the police station, the boys overhear those telephone calls, plus one to the coastguard. Sergeant Hopkins says, 'Boys, you can go home now.' They hurry from the police station towards town.

'You know what this means?' Willy says. 'We must go back tonight to suss out The Crags.' Ted and Daks nod in keen agreement.

'We gotta tell the girls,' Daks says.

~

The police news is spread within the hour by the town's gossips. Kate, Yoko and Sharon, wearing their netball uniforms, race up to the three boys.

'Was the body all gross and bloated?' Yoko demands.

Sharon pinches her nose. 'Must've been stinky?'

Kate glares at the boys. 'Well, tell us.'

Daks says, 'The policeman said it looked like a dead body, but it wasn't.'

Puzzled, Sharon looks at Yoko, who shrugs. Kate

understands, she says, 'When are we going back to The Crags?'

'Tonight,' Willy confirms. 'No sleeping in, Daks.' They all laugh. 'Oh, it's still a big moon tonight.'

'Very spooky.' Sharon puts her hands to her sunburnt cheeks.

'You're acting very silly,' Ted says. 'Know something we don't?'

Sharon grins, does a cartwheel. They begin to disperse. Kate calls to them, 'Don't forget to bring your detective ID's.'

~

Five minutes to eleven on Saturday night. Everyone slips away from their bedrooms. The Milky Way stars sparkle. Moonlight helps them to make good time. Soon, they again set up their spy camp on top of The Crags lookout. Between them, they now have three pairs of binoculars to share.

'Goody, goody,' says Sharon, as Daks pours hot chocolate drinks from a thermos flask. Daks keeps his secret that it was his mum who made the hot drinks. Kate hands out sandwiches.

Willy cups his hands to his ears. 'Where's them strange noises coming from?'

'Shush, Willy,' Kate says. 'I'm trying to listen.'

Yoko uses her torch to check the time. She whispers in Kate's ear. Kate updates the spy logbook.

'My dad told me noise travels further over water at night,' Ted says.

Willy frowns. 'Yeah, I know that.'

Ted turns about. 'Aah! Sounds like a tractor engine down on the dunes.'

Quick as a flash, Daks swings his legs over the top verge. 'Come on, I'll be lead scout.' He slides down on his backside into the scrub far below. Ted follows him.

Yoko instructs Kate, 'Jot something down.'

Willy munches on another sandwich. He peers over the edge. 'Can't see 'em, too dark,' he mumbles. The girls, each using binoculars, resume looking out to sea for any sign of the mysterious lights.

~

Daks and Ted join up at the foot of the escarpment. They scramble over the sand dunes, crawling towards the mechanical sounds: throb, throb, throb.

'Come on,' Daks encourages, 'let's get closer.' Soon they hide behind low scrub and keep quite still.

Ted nudges Daks, points towards a faint dome of light. 'There's somethin' parked across the high tide-line.' They edge closer.

Daks whispers, 'It's a big tow truck farting diesel fumes.'

'Phew,' Ted wrinkles his nose.

'Can you see where's the tow cable going?'

Ted leans forward, scans the beach. 'It stretches way over, past the rocks. They're tryin' to pull somethin' heavy from the sea. The cable's straining, must be tangled.'

'There's lots of kelp beds out there,' Daks says. 'Geeze. Be great if it's pirate treasure and skeletons.'

'You reckon?'

'Just kidding.' Daks smirks.

Ted whispers, 'Look-see, two blokes.'

'The winchman, I know him.' Daks strains to see better. 'It's Mr McGooly from the fishing co-op. Dad thinks he's a drongo.'

'Who's da bloke in shorts, using the flashlight?'

'Can't see his face,' Daks says. 'Wait on, it's what's-his-name.'

'Who, Daks?'

'That chicken farmer, works up the back paddock, behind Miss Cutty's house. I've seen him hanging about the co-op. Sometimes works as a deckhand. Reckon they hid the dinghy?'

'Shush, Daks.'

'They won't hear us over the din of the motor,' Daks snaps.

'Could be smugglers?' Ted wonders aloud.

Daks dry swallows. 'We'll soon see, unless the lights go out.'

Ted nudges Daks. 'Want to sneak down, let the tyres down?'

'No way! They'll catch us, and bury us up to our necks in sand. Geeze, the tide will come in, and we'll be goners.'

Ted sits bolt upright, pulls a scared face. 'Wish we had some of your hot chocolate to drink.'

Mr McGooly spots Ted's sudden movement. He shines his torch. 'Hey. Get out of here, scram!' He rushes towards their hideout, stumbles on-all-fours before them, looks up. 'Go on, scram!' Scared, Ted and Daks jump to their feet, and scramble up the cliff face like hermit crabs.

~

'Wow-ee!' Kate cries. 'Heaps of bright lights. Some yellow, some red, and one flashing bright green.' She scribbles notes into the logbook.

'Won't everyone in town see 'em?' Willy says. 'There must be two or three boats out there?' They hear men's voices carried by the fresh sea breeze.

Kate asks Yoko, 'What's the time now?'

Yoko shines her torch. 'Five minutes to three.'

Sharon rubs her eyes. 'Town's fast asleep, and soon, me, too.'

The illuminated patch of sea begins to bubble and froth. The coloured lights sway every which way. Willy says, 'It's like watching a submarine movie.'

'Fantastical,' Yoko chirps. 'We'll be famous tomorrow for solving the mystery of the lights.'

The mesmerised group jumps out of their skins when Ted and Daks surge over the rim. Ted, puffing, begins to explain the cable set-up below, but stops as an ear piercing sound reverberates. The tow-cable snaps, whips backwards, smacking into the truck's cabin, and flattens the surrounding foliage. Followed by cries of Argh! Argh! Argh!

They all peer over the edge towards the dome of light. Daks's and Ted's eyes focus first, they exchange worried glances.

'Mr McGooly's rolling about,' Ted says, 'clutching his

leg.'

'Yuk, lots of blood!' Daks tells. 'I better go get help.'

'No way, I'm faster,' Ted says. 'I'll fetch the Doc.' He grabs a torch, and races away.

The children refocus on the mysterious coloured lights. A giant monster of the deep rises through kelp tentacles. The girls stand up, holding hands in stunned silence. Willy is mesmerised as a bulbous object, pitching and rocking, pops to the surface. 'A huge sea monster,' he cries. 'Looks real dangerous.'

'Just like *Moby Dick's* white whale,' Kate says.

'More like *20,000 Leagues Under the Sea*,' Sharon says, 'that we saw at the flicks.'

'Shaz, it's not the *Nautilus*,' Daks says, watching through binoculars. 'It's the hull of a fishing boat. Lots of barnacles, gooey slime, and huge air-bubbles.'

'Fantastical!' Yoko squeals, squeezing the girls' hands.

A coastguard vessel approaches, circles the cluster of smaller salvage boats. A powerful searchlight illuminates the bobbing ship's upturned hull. More of the shipwreck is revealed as sea water pours from its wheelhouse and broken portholes. The children cheer 'hooray, hooray, hooray' when they hear a distant ambulance siren. Help is on the way for Mr McGooly.

Daybreak peeks over the horizon. The local newspaper headline reads: *Sunken trawler, Gypsy Rose, found.*

~

After a big sleep-in and lots of parental quizzing and tricky explaining, the excited children gather at their primary school's shelter shed. Kate reads out the last Club Ozity logbook entry:

Mystery Lights at Sea

Case Solved: Five minutes to six, Sunday morning, 21 October 1956

Big Moon. High Tide. Swift Current

The Crags lookout. Compass bearing SWW

Fishing trawler, *Gypsy Rose,* missing since Easter, raised from sunken grave

Coastguard captures salvage boats. Pirates arrested

Man injured, broken leg, recovering in hospital

Police Sergeant Hopkins praises us for our witness statements

~

Five minutes to three in the afternoon. Kate glances at Yoko's watch, 'Case closed'.

The Howling

Ingrid Fry

A screaming comes across the sky.[5] The mournful wail is relentless. The howl ebbs and flows on the wind, its sad refrain filled with despair. Boo and Schmoo are disturbed by the sound as well. Two unhappy beagles lock their big brown eyes with mine, pleading for me to do *something*.

We set off late in the evening. Boo, Schmoo and I were on a mission to find the source of the howling. The poor dog has been crying for days. Something must be done.

Back and forth, up, down and around the dark streets

[5] First line from *Gravity's Rainbow*, Thomas Pynchon

we walk. The wind pulls the cry hither and thither, making it tricky to pin down the exact location.

Boo and Schmoo are keen on one particular property perched atop a steep slope. Noses sniff the air as they pull on their leads and drag me towards it.

The dilapidated house sits in darkness, nestled amid a garden overgrown with weeds. Windows, like black hooded eyes, stare down at us. The broken palings of a white picket fence surround us with what looks like a sinister smile of jagged teeth. We sneak down the driveway towards the backyard. The howling intensifies as we draw closer. It's as if the poor creature knows help is at hand.

'Well done, girls,' I whisper. 'We've nailed it. The sound's definitely coming from here.'

It was nearly midnight, too late, and too creepy, to do anything. Tomorrow, I'd go back and knock on that door.

The next day dawns, and everything is quiet in the 'hood. It's as though our visit put the wind up them. Maybe the dog had been moved?

That night, however, it starts again. The peace of our suburb is cruelly punctuated by a pitiful, monotonous yowling.

'I've had enough! I'm going back to that damn house.'

Jason, my partner, gives me a look. 'Maggie, you shouldn't go on your own, it's not safe.'

'I won't be on my own. Boo and Schmoo will be with me.'

'Yeah, great, two vicious beagles—that'll really scare

the daylights out of someone.'

'Well, you come then.'

'You know I don't like to get involved in neighbourhood disputes. Just call me if you need backup.'

'How come I always have to do the dirty work?'

He laughs. 'Because you're good at it.'

'Hmmpf.'

Boo, Schmoo and I kit up and set off to investigate. I bring along their heavy-duty ball thrower. It has a long, sturdy handle which can double as a whacking stick if things turn ugly.

Walking briskly, we soon reach the suspect house. Light shines dimly through the glass in the front door. Ah ha! Someone's home. I don't want to appear intimidating, so I stash the heavy-duty ball thrower near the lopsided mail box.

We pick our way carefully along the broken bluestone pathway to the front door. I look for a doorbell. There is none. Just a ginormous brass doorknocker. I use it.

Bang! Bang! Bang!

The sound echoes through the night. We listen for a response. I feel my heartbeat ramp up to high.

Heavy footsteps make their way towards the door. The porch light comes on. The door opens.

He's six foot four and built like a tank. A very fat tank. An unkempt beard, blue singlet, and hideous tattoos complete the picture. My sense of bravado and moral outrage rapidly evaporate.

He grunts at me. '*What?*'

I use my most polite, and non-threatening voice. 'Um, I was wondering if that's your dog barking or your neighbours?'

He wipes his bulbous nose with the back of his hand. 'It's mine. What of it, bitch?'

'Well, it sounds unhappy, and it's keeping the whole neighbourhood awake.'

He lunges forward, grabs my T-shirt, and twists it up tight around my neck. He pulls my face close to his tobacco stained, food encrusted beard.

'So, watcha gonna do about it, girlie?'

A stench of dental decay, tobacco and bourbon wafts across my face.

'This!' I say, as I jam my bony knee hard into his groin. A blast of rank air explodes from his lungs as he gasps in pain. His knees buckle and his grip loosens. I push him back and ram my elbow into his solar plexus. Tank man hits the ground like a sack of spuds. My karate teacher would be proud! Boo leaps onto his fat gut, and balances on his jelly belly. Her face is a snarling display of shiny white teeth as she stares him down, ready to rip out his throat if he so much as blinks. Bad-ass Boo the beagle. Huh. Who knew?

We freeze, and listen, waiting for any cronies to appear. No one does. It looks like tank man's the only one home.

Schmoo and I hightail it through the house, searching for the dog. Following the sound of the howling, we fly down two flights of stairs, and find ourselves in a man cave. Adorning the room is a pool table, mirrored bar with surfboard tabletop, stools with Coca Cola bottle-top seats, and a hideous, curved, red velvet couch. At the end of the room are glass doors, through which I see a shed at the end of the backyard. The howling is coming from there.

Quickly, and quietly, we make our way to the shed. A light is on, so I peep in through a hole in the window covering. A stink, like cat urine and fertiliser, fills the air. Schmoo gives an explosive sneeze. I drag her back and hide in the bushes. We wait. I hold my breath. No one comes out.

I go back to the window and take another peek.

Glass jars, rubber tubing, masks, filters, strainers, respiratory masks and containers of multi-layered liquids cover stainless steel benches. I haven't watched the entire series of *Breaking Bad* for nothing. I know what I'm looking at. A meth lab. Right here, in the leafy outer suburbs of Melbourne.

I jump in fright as a bloodshot, brown eyeball peers back at me. It's the dog!

We have to save the poor thing. I try the door. It's locked. A birdbath is nearby. I slide off the bowl, pick up the base, and ram it into the door lock.

The door flies open, a little Schnauzer dashes out, and spins in crazy, happy circles at my feet.

'Come on pup, we're busting you outta here!'

We run back into the house, up the stairs, and head for the front door. Tank man is still on the floor groaning, with Boo snarling into his face.

I leap over him. 'Let's go, girls!'

Schmoo gives tank man a complimentary nip on the way past. The little Schnauzer pauses, cocks his leg, and pisses into his earhole.

'Nice work, little one,' I say, as the four of us flee into the night.

Safely home, with the authorities notified, I grab a glass of red wine and join the three dogs curled up in front of the fire. We stare into the flames and enjoy the newly restored peace and quiet of our 'burb.

Where There's Life, There's Hope

Ingrid Fry

The sky above the port was the colour of television, tuned to a dead channel.[6] Kyra averted her gaze from the dismal greyness. She stared in disbelief at the life support system that had sustained her agelessly for two hundred and sixty years, yet had failed to do the same for her partner.

The shrunken body of Nova lay entombed in his silicone capsule. His face, dehydrated and shrivelled, was fixed in an expression of terror and despair. For him, the

6 First line from Neuromancer, William Gibson.

experiment in suspended animation had failed.

'Attention, please.'

Kyra strapped herself down as REM, the computer, pleasantly announced the commencement of re-entry.

Her mind raced. How much had Earth changed? How well could she adapt without Nova's support? A cold and silent terror gripped her. Breathing deeply, she tried to calm herself.

Re-entry and landing was smooth and routine. Kyra unbuckled and switched on the receiver. No transmission. She frowned and carefully adjusted the controls. The quiet hum of the pod seemed to be the only sound in existence.

She pressed the button to withdraw the outer shielding. 'Let's get a visual.'

Outside, the shielding drew back like a huge eyelid. Kyra started in fright at the scene revealed before her.

'My God. Where am I?'

'Earth,' REM said.

A burning point of panic grew in the pit of her stomach.

'REM, give me a complete analysis of atmosphere, and check landing coordinates.'

'One moment, please.'

Black glass and mist. Kyra's mind struggled to comprehend. Earth had no landscape like this.

'Atmosphere breathable, landing coordinates correct. Sensors indicate low-level radiation, suggest protective gear be worn when disembarking.'

Kyra read REM's analysis, fighting off a strong feeling of unreality. The facts were before her. The area had been hit by a nuclear blast so powerful, the land became molten, eventually cooling and fusing into the black glassy substance she saw outside. Her eyes blinked back tears as she read the report's clinical summation: *No indication of life.*

'Not even a cockroach, REM?'

'Negative.'

~

The terrain was treacherous. Kyra moved cautiously, fearful of the jagged edges of rock all around. Her destination was a hill, from which she hoped to be able to view the surrounding area. She felt completely numb. Her mind, shocked and dazed, refused to function. Only one emotion filtered through—sharp, tragic and insane in its intensity—a desire to find something still living. It drove her on. Stumbling, half crawling, she finally reached the summit. Her eyes strained, desperate to see through the mist.

Kyra's suit began to ripple and she realised a wind had sprung up. Gradually, the atmosphere became clearer, and she perceived shapes in the distance which differed to the terrain she had covered. Resembling huge blackened tree stumps, the city's buildings rose up before her. The sun reflected on the broken and twisted metal, and for a moment she paused, awed at the sight of this huge metropolis, so strange and beautiful in its desolation.

~

Kyra picked her way through the debris of the deserted streets. The silence preyed on her mind. It was as if the city was focusing its attention on her—an intruder. The blackened buildings seemed malevolent, leaning closer, whispering, hunching over to peer at her with baleful, reflective eyes. Objects seemed to dart and move in the corners of her vision and she found herself turning quickly to try and catch them.

The sun disappeared as the buildings dragged a shawl of mist down around their shoulders, and the wind, tired of tugging at her suit, became completely still.

Kyra realised she should seek shelter for the night, and stepped bravely into the jaws of a nearby ruin. The sound of her footsteps seemed deafening as she hurriedly looked for a corner in which to sleep. She curled up under a large piece of concrete, and stared out into the darkness, as the silence settled around her ears.

That night her dreams were filled with darkness and despair, death and decay. On awakening, the lust for some contact with life caused her physical pain.

She sat in the dust and rubble and watched a ray of sunshine creep slowly through a hole in the wall. It gave her some comfort, a welcome relief and contrast from the endless blackness. The ray moved slowly, the darkness seeming to resist its intrusion.

On the ground, a patch of yellow flared up brighter than the ray itself. She rose slowly to her feet and made her way towards the enticing colour. A warmth rushed through Kyra's body, her face flushed, and tears welled in her eyes. Gently, so gently, afraid it may vanish, she picked up the bowl containing a fragile embodiment of colour—a flower.

Something had survived! Her heart thumped in her chest with the joy of it. Carefully packing the soil back around its stem, she held the flower up to her face plate, her soul drinking in the translucent beauty of that single flower. Such delicate petals, the stem, green and healthy, bristled with fine hairs, each leaf, vein, and bud radiated vitality. Kyra was euphoric, transported by her delight and reverence for this most precious piece of life.

Cradling the bowl, Kyra moved towards the exit, her eyes fixed on the flower's gay radiance. She didn't see the loose flooring until it was too late. Falling heavily, a steel rod pierced her suit and embedded itself in her chest.

Consciousness was slipping away with her life's blood. She reached out desperately for the plant which had rolled just out of reach. Pain receded as she finally grasped the flower and brought it towards her. 'Oh, my beauty. With life, there's hope.'

As Kyra drank in its loveliness for the last time, a fine slip of white attached to the stem caught her eye. Her fingers, clumsy in the suit, pulled it away and she saw it was inscribed with tiny print. A crushing horror overcame her as she deciphered the tag—*Daffodil. Reality Synthetics. Made in China.*

Same Thing, No Difference

Sakuntala Gananathan

Our hero was not one of those Dominican cats everybody's always going on about—he wasn't no home-runner hitter or a fly bachatero, not a playboy with a million hots on his jock because he was seven then.[7]

It was mid-morning in late spring and the invitees hurried to take a seat in the enormous assembly hall. Their dress code ranged from formal suits, to casual wear, to unstitched material carelessly wrapped around half-

[7] First line from *The Brief Wondrous Life of Oscar Wao*, Junot Diaz

naked bodies. Some ambled in with flip-flops, while one young woman walked in barefooted.

The conference table was round so that none could take precedence over another. Was it King Arthur's Round Table wondered a man who appeared equally ancient. The chairs were of identical shape and size to prevent any one of them from claiming a status higher than another.

It was unanimously agreed to let the oldest member inaugurate the session with a brief introduction of his subject matter. He would then be followed by the person on his right until each one of them had had an opportunity to give a clue of what he or she was going to discuss at length over the course of the day.

While most scriptures were written in horizontal lines, with words running from left to right, there were some texts starting from extreme right to left. Yet a few were compositions in brushstrokes, flowing down vertical columns with each new column beginning to the left of the one preceding. There were a couple of oral works which had survived the ravages of time thanks to disciples committing them to memory and passing the same down to their followers. Although there was a move to get these published, it was resisted by the more orthodox members, who preferred to chant the stanzas so as not to obliterate the nuances in tone and meaning.

One man said his was the best course to adopt. While he enlarged on the divine aspects of his belief, another browbeat him. 'My own path is sublime, profound, and the shortest way for salvation.'

'Salvation? No. Deliverance? Yes,' insisted the man next to him.

'While praying, raise your head.'

'No,' objected the lady in mauve. 'Bow down in reverence.'

'Nonsense! Kneel down and pray with your eyes closed.'

'Oh, no! Stand up and look into the heavens above.'

'Prostrate on the floor and pray with arms stretched above your head.'

'Join palms together.'

Their beliefs were as diverse as their apparel and soon voices rose in protest. Over one matter, however, there was consensus. All agreed that good should prevail and evil spurned.

~

Everyone sighed with relief on finding a pivotal point upon which to continue the conference. Alas, it didn't last for long and presently their voices again reached a crescendo.

~

Seven-year-old Tom running past the venue happened to overhear them. Overcome with curiosity he peeped over a hedge of azaleas outside a window.

Their discussions went back and forth, with each driving a point, immediately prompting the next person to squash the preceding speaker's conviction to smithereens. They spoke off-the-cuff or read from books ancient and modern, while a handful chanted their sacred learning, pausing after each stanza so that translators could enlighten the rest of them.

Standing about ten feet behind the speakers were their followers, committing to memory every word their mentors uttered.

And so, the morning wore on until lunch-time, whereupon the delegates—not their followers or translators—retired to the dining room.

A wide array of salads, sandwiches, and bread rolls were attractively displayed on long counters. Tables were laid with bowls of steamed rice, couscous, pasta and noodles, besides various preparations of vegetables, eggs, fish and meat, with spice and without.

There were those who used forks in their left hand, or right, but nobody commented, not even when some used their fingers to roll up their food and place it in their mouths. Two of them sat down on the floor, as was their custom, and ate in silence. Quite a number deftly used chopsticks to shovel their noodles, while none pursed their lips on hearing a man slurp noodles from his bowl.

For dessert, several picked puddings and ice cream of numerous flavours, while others had a choice of strawberries and peaches; with or without fresh cream; grapes, bananas, apples, and dried nuts, plain or soaked in honey. The display was sumptuous, and the guests had more than a couple of serves of their favourites.

A separate mention needs to be made of durian, a

spiky fruit like a jackfruit, but smaller in size. It has a pungent smell, but otherwise, it is fit for a king. It was not found in the fruit platters but was placed at a safe distance so as not to put off those with sensitive nostrils: the owners of such nostrils were, however, amused to find a couple of takers for the nauseating fruit.

'What made you choose kiwi fruit?' asked a man, savouring a slice of mango and reaching for another.

'I love the taste of kiwi in my mouth. Do you know it's the most nutritious fruit in the world?'

'I understand that papaya is recommended for everyone, including diabetics,' said a well-built man, scooping out half the fruit.

'Well, an apple a day keeps the doctor away,' one was heard to say as he bit into a red delicious.

Indeed, overall it was an enjoyable meal, and each ate whatever they wished at their own pace and nobody objected, raised an eyebrow or curled their lip in disgust.

~

Presently, they retired to the conference room and resumed their debate. However, unlike in the morning, most suffered from fatigue, while a couple of them felt light-headed and yet a few had muscle cramps.

Tom came into the hall on the pretext of retrieving his ball which he had kicked underneath the table. He was troubled to find the crowd looking quite worn out. Sitting down on the floor, he brought out an iPad from his backpack. After a few minutes, he walked up to the nearest delegate and whispered into his ear, 'How about some abba?'

'Well, I hear ABBA returned after 35 years with two new songs.'

The boy laughed aloud and asked the next person, 'Would you like to have nero?'

'Thanks, I am fine. I have had a full meal and any mention of food makes me queasy.'

'How about some wai?' he asked the next delegate.

The man had never heard of the word. Feeling dizzy, he took the easy way out by shutting his eyes.

'How about having vodo?' the young chap asked a woman in a bikini.

'No, thank you,' she said, not wishing to admit her ignorance.

'Did you say aflaj?' asked the half-naked man. 'I have set opinions and wouldn't wish to try out anything strange or new.'

'Would you like to have shui, Madam?'

The elderly woman pretended not to have noticed him and removed her hearing aid. *It's sufficient embarrassment for me to seek my grandson's help to get my laptop working* she thought.

'Shui?' a man in boxer shorts repeated. 'I'm pretty sure I won't need it.'

By the time Tom had gone around the circular table, he, too, felt exhausted. He rummaged through his bag for his bottle of water and took a long gulp.

Immediately, there was a babble of voices calling out for aqua, shui, wasser, eau, jal, nero, mayim, thanneer, abba, agua, vatura, pani, aflaj, appos, vodo and so forth. They scrambled over the polished table top to get at least a drop of the liquid. Each called out in his native dialect and each had a gulp of water to quench his thirst.

Whatever name they called it by, they all meant the same thing.

Same thing; no difference. Same difference.

Fortitude

Margaret Hepworth

We have been lost to each other for so long.[8]

South Africa, Robben Island, 1972

'It's all about language!' Mandela stated firmly. His jailer regarded him inquiringly. 'Take yourself for instance, Dirk. Some would call you my captor.' The hapless Dirk began a feeble interjection, but Mandela had not finished. 'I'm not calling you my captor, Dirk. I am calling you a victim of circumstance. And you know, my friend, I forgave you a long time ago.' Mandela spoke consolingly,

---

[8] First line from *The Red Tent,* Anita Diamant

patting the gun-laden Dirk on the shoulder.

Dirk Kortella had found himself in the most remarkable of circumstances. As a young nineteen-year-old, loyal to his President and country, Dirk had joined South African Internal Security with the surety and certainty of youth, knowing that truth was on his side. When the African National Congress had declared they would 'bring the system down' he understood this to be treason. When Nelson Mandela, the enigmatic leader of the ANC had been captured, Dirk had celebrated, toasting with his colleagues; 'the bastard's finally gone under!'

So to find himself, nine long years later, in full-fledged daily discussion with the man himself, sharing thoughts and philosophies in a lonely cell the size of a boot box, was what Dirk had jokingly pointed out to Mandela, an 'Almost Impossible Thought.'

'Nelson, if anyone had said to me only twelve months ago, next year you will be sitting with Mandela chewing over life and liberty, I would have seriously punched his lights out. Yet look at us now.'

'Dirk, if anyone said it to you today, you would still deny it!'

It was true, and for that Dirk was ashamed; the fact that he could not tell the truth to his friends, family, even his own wife, was Dirk's greatest source of humiliation and cause for repentance. But he found himself captive within his own dilemma. In apartheid-ridden South Africa, even going to the confessional at his local Dutch

Reformist Church could lay Dirk wide open to charges of an unfathomable nature.

For now, both he and Nelson chose to keep their conversations between themselves.

'Pray continue, Nelson. Tell me about language as the be all and end all, as you say!' His Afrikaner accent rang around the hollow cell.

'It is through our thoughts that we create our reality. It is through our language, the way we choose to express those thoughts, that we most greatly influence others in society.'

'Yes, well that's obvious, Nelson. A great orator has the power of enormous persuasion and influence.'

'True,' agreed his friend. 'But I am talking about something far more insidious and pervasive. It is the everyday language of the layman that constructs our reality.'

Mandela paused to think for a moment, rubbing at his neatly cropped dark beard as he was want to do when deep in reflective thought.

'Take for example the language surrounding the "Conflict in Vietnam". A "*conflict*", Dirk, really? An undeclared invasion of another country labeled a "conflict". Government rhetoric at its best! But it's when the public chooses to accept it, to take it on, to own it. That's when it becomes problematic. A "*conflict*",' he repeated indignantly. 'See how it diminishes the severity of what is going on over there. The Americans are involved in a "conflict", with Ho Chi Minh, a conflict that just happens to involve the killing of thousands of innocents.

'And again, my young friend, stop and think. Let's bring this conversation closer to home. You are now speaking with, perhaps *colluding* with, a terrorist.' He paused, a cheeky look in his eyes, taunting the younger man now, playing to his fears. His face turned suddenly serious. 'Dirk, to many I am a freedom fighter.'

Dirk sighed. Initially, he had hated Mandela. How could he not? Dirk was born and bred Afrikaner; born into the apartheid system and a proud product of it. When he first laid eyes on Mandela, shackled, shuffling, adorned in the same khaki, shabby uniform of all the Robben Island prisoners, Dirk could have spat on him and everything he represented. Mandela didn't look so tough. The African National Congress had sworn to sabotage; Mandela himself had admitted to such plans. But over time, as Dirk had observed Mandela, something served to change him. And he began to understand just who Mandela was and the unconventional power he wielded. For no matter how much hatred was thrown his way, literally taunted in his face, Mandela never failed to maintain his composure and his dignity. Fortitude in the face of inhumanity. Dirk had been close by when his colleague had accosted Mandela. A freshly cut key plunged and held deep in the folds of Mandela's throat. The pulsating vein only millimetres below the skin. Mandela had spoken quietly, confronting the jailer's blue eyes with his own deep brown. 'If you tear open my throat with that key you will effectively unlock every door on every cell in this barren, forsaken prison. I'm not so sure that you want that to happen.' The jailer's face had contorted into a palette of immeasurable hate. He hawked loudly and spat in Mandela's face before straightening and moving on.

Slowly, Dirk's eyes had been awakened to the brutality that existed within the system. His system! It was he who ventured the first move towards friendship, offering Mandela a stick of gum.

Now they sat yet again together, hidden by the solitary nature of Mandela's cell. And Mandela continued with this, his latest theorising.

'I come to my main lesson for the day, young Dirk, so listen carefully. We are talking about the common use of language and its influence on our thinking. When we use the word "man" we speak of one man, one person of the male persuasion, such as yourself. When we replace the lower case "m" with a capital, we are now speaking of …'

'Man, as in all men,' ventured Dirk, hesitantly. He was never quite sure where Mandela was headed in these conversations and he didn't like to appear foolish.

Mandela raised one eyebrow.

'Oh and all women too, of course!'

'Yes, quite right, Dirk,' Mandela praised his young companion. 'The word Man has been used in all manner of texts, including religious dissertations, political documents, scientific journals and so on. For me there are several problems with the connotations of such a word. The fact that it precludes women, for a start. Yes, I know the capital supposedly allows for all people to be taken into account, but let's face it Dirk, by its very sound in common speech it still flavours our brains with a distinctly male taste. The other reason I object to its use is this. Listen carefully to the word. "Man". Although plural, again a consequence of its capitalisation, it strikes us as singular. It sounds as though we stand alone. In isolation. Even collectively as a group, it allows us no connectivity with other groups upon this earth.'

Dirk could see Mandela's point. When he played with the word in his head it was precisely as Mandela pointed out. 'How about "Mankind" then?'

'Yes, I had thought of that too. The connotations are certainly better. Myself, I am hoping we can replace the noun by using the word "Humanity". Think about it Dirk. If every political document referred to Humanity. Instead of "All Men are created equal" we would read "All Humanity is equal". Where would we find ourselves now if we discussed "The evolution of Humanity"? If the Bible stated "And God made Humanity", we'd be forced by the very way our brains accept language, to think as a collective. To think beyond ourselves, hopefully even beyond the group. Dirk, this is thought in extension!'

Suddenly, Mandela's demeanour changed, his voice lowered and sorrow laced the older man's tone. 'I'm fearful, Dirk.' The young officer looked up quickly. Fear was a word he rarely, if ever, heard Mandela use. 'I look around me at my fellow inmates. I watch their suffering as they are isolated from family, friends, loved ones. Feeling so forsaken, wretched. I fear they are losing their belief, their faith in the existence of God.'

'Perhaps, Nelson,' said Dirk, contemplatively eyeing the barren cell, the cold iron barring Mandela's physical freedom, his own blood-stained truncheon such as was cheerfully carried by all security guards, 'perhaps instead of pondering the existence of God, we should be questioning the existence of Humanity?'

The key snapped in the lock and Dirk, head down, turned slowly away. It was difficult to face his life now. He despised the system that held men like Mandela captive; the very system in which he continued to play a key role. Maybe one day, things will change; 'An Almost Impossible Thought.' Still pondering Mandela's words, he headed on to the officers' apartments, back to his wife and young child.

What a Coincidence

Marlene Laurent

If you wish strongly enough for something it will come true, perhaps not exactly as you have envisaged it, but it will come true.[9]

Prisoner-of-War Camp, Germany, 1942

I saw it out of the corner of my eye. The hot sun shone on something buried in the dirt. My curiosity got the better of me. Looking around to see if anybody was watching I walked slowly towards the spot trying not to draw attention to myself. These days I was hungry most of the time, and had lost weight. My clothes hung on my

9 First line from *View from a Barred Window*, Katharina Fares

body and my bones were visible through my skin. Life was hell on earth.

Squatting on the ground I began to dig the soil away to uncover it. Realising it was a brass object lying on its side I became quite excited; something that hadn't happened in a long time, not since coming to the POW camp. After some frantic digging my hands were getting tired. Finally, I lifted the object out of the ground. It was about ten and half inches long and cylindrical in shape. I knew straight away what it was as I had been a gunner. I'd watched the artillery shells fall out of the cannons as we fired at the enemy. The stutter of guns firing at the enemy rang in my ears—the heat and dirt were all around me again.

Hiding the object in my loose clothes, I ambled back to my hut. Sitting down on my bed I unwrapped my find and, using a corner of my flimsy clothes to clean the dirt off the bottom of the shell casing, I managed to read that the it had been manufactured in July 1917. Hiding it under my bed I thought about what I could do with it. My mind began to wander. Then I remembered my trip to Cairo when on leave.

Camels were ambling down the busy laneway, people were haggling over the produce of the day—the smell of fish was pungent and made me want to throw up. Beautiful women were gliding past me, their faces covered with colourful scarves. Cairo was exciting, and for a country boy from Australia, it was like walking into another world. For a day I forgot about the war and drifted into the life of an Egyptian.

Image of the arterial shell the story is based on.

Making my way to the museum I became engrossed looking at artefacts of rare beauty and colour. Tutankhamen's gold funerary mask was exquisite and shone as a bright memory for me. At the museum, I bought a book about the pharaohs and read about their obsession with the afterlife. This was a poignant reminder for me that I was not likely to live beyond the war. Most of my battalion were wounded or dead. Thousands of lives were taken in an instant. *They* were not afforded the opportunity of having luxuries in the afterlife. Bodies were left lying to rot or thrown into a deep pit. Occasionally we had time to bury our mates with a simple service and a cross made from the branch of a tree. No exotic things to surround them or me in the next life. My tomb would be simple but meaningful. It would house my mummified horse and dog, my riding saddle, blanket, and boots, as well as my grandfather's watch and chain, given to me when he died. Toss in a billy and packet of tea to and I would be happy.

Bottom view of the shell

Suddenly snapping out of my daydream I decided that I would engrave something that would remind me of that beautiful day in Cairo. Carving the historical records of the days of the Egyptian pharaohs kept my mind active. So began a daily ritual of engraving. Despite hunger and listlessness, I dragged my skeleton down to the back of the complex, out of sight of the guards, to work on my masterpiece and forget the hunger, the pain from weeping ulcers on my legs and the fear of dying. Being one of the lucky ones my wish came true. I survived that hell hole. As we were herded out of the gate and made our way to the hospital base I didn't even give my now completed Egyptian engraved artillery shell a thought.

Andre's farm, Belgium, 1948

The tractor lurched forward chugging along over the undulating Belgian fields. The smell of freshly turned earth heralded the beginning of spring. Icy cold winds whispered their goodbyes, as occasional falls of snow became less frequent. Hope and prosperity replaced fear and despair from war times. The fields were ripe and beckoning me to plant new crops. Visions of soldiers lying on their bellies, crawling forward towards the enemy, frequently flashed into my mind. The constant stutter of guns fired endlessly killing thousands, their ghostly voices echoing across the field that provided a grave for the many dead. The sun, pushing its rays from between two clouds, gave an eerie sense of the afterlife.

Clunk! The tractor lurched forward then stalled. I jumped off to see what had caused it. I saw something glinting, almost winking at me, in the sun. Skulls of the dead haunted me but it was a relief to discover an artillery shell, a large artillery shell. It asked me to pick it up and although it was caked with dirt I tossed it in my backpack, the weight of it almost whispered to me that it had been the facilitator of death.

Darkness crept up and enveloped our tiny house and as I wearily changed my clothes curiosity got the better of me. 'Found this in the fields today', I mumbled to my wife, Marie. The etchings were barely visible, so I handed it to Marie who began to rub it clean with the corner of her apron. Like a genie the etchings came to life telling of another culture and time. As she tipped the shell, I noted the date engraved on the base—July 1917. My creaky old chair which had somehow survived night raids and day skirmishes comforted and enveloped me as I wearily dozed after dinner.

Awakening from my slumber I once again saw the glint of the artillery shell. Staring silently in the semi-gloom, it became alive with its beautifully engraved markings depicting pyramids. The fire threw eerie shadows across the walls and pharaohs spoke to me. Lost in my dreams I was a slave building a pyramid for a pharaoh to store objects hewn in gold and precious stones.

The next morning the cold air woke me, and I was jolted back into a world that called me to provide for us. But the engravings had had a profound effect on me, wanting me to evaluate the meaning of life and the ghosts of the many who had died during the war. The after-life was just as important as the here and now. I realised that this belief was in sharp contrast to my own pagan beliefs, that there is no after-life. Although there were many amazing and beautiful artefacts stored in the pyramids they too had had their day, plundered by people from other countries, like thieves in the night.

The artillery shell became an intricate part of our lives. Each week Marie found some flowers or greenery to put in it. So it became a sort of ritual, allowing us to honour the memory of brave friends who had fought and died to give us a world that accepted all races, beliefs and religions.

Marie and I were survivors and had seen many horrors in our short lives. We were married just before the war began and had not had children—although we wished for them. The years rolled by, and the seasons came and went. One cold winter's day when Marie was replacing the dead twigs with fresh greenery she turned to me and smiled.

'What?' I said.

'I am pregnant', was her reply. I grasped her in my arms and we hugged and danced around the kitchen.

Once we had recovered from our excitement I looked at her and said, 'Today three years ago, I found the artillery shell'. As we embraced I contemplated the coincidence. Neither of us could explain how we felt. It was almost as if the rubbing of the vase had let the genie out of the bottle. Seven months later I heard the cry of a beautiful little baby boy. We decided to call him Pepi after Pepi II, a pharaoh from the sixth dynasty who ruled Egypt for the longest time—ninety-four years. We wanted longevity for our son.

I was sitting by the window when Pepi arrived. He

was now a young man, tall and lean. It had been seven years since he met and married his wife. Both of them had given us so much joy, including, two grandchildren, a boy and a girl. My grey hair was now sparse and my eyesight dim. How the years had flown. Marie was no longer with me, although everything in our house reminded me of her and how happy we had been before the cancer stole her away from me. Now I was alone. I no longer worked in the fields and spent my days pottering around the property. Pepi had come to talk to me about moving in with them, and in the end, I had agreed.

As we were packing up the family items I saw something glinting in the corner and recognised it as the artillery shell I had found many years earlier. After years of neglect it was no longer shiny and bright. I couldn't recall exactly when our ritual had stopped. It was packed into one of the many boxes and I don't know what happened to it. I never saw it again.

London, 1963

Katie was quirky. She liked to dress in bright colours and was never a slave to fashion. Her favourite pastime was to collect items from jumble sales to take home. She loved haggling and her weekends were spent buying food for the week and looking for treasures. As she wandered along past the tables the items displayed spoke to her of other owners and times. Old jewellery, crockery and books had unwritten stories to tell. Her vivid imagination would take her thoughts to another time, another place.

Perusing items on the table she saw something glinting in the sun. At first, she wondered what it could be and asked the peddler if she could have a closer look. Unsure as to what it was, she inquired about its age.

'Look on the bottom. It says it was manufactured in July 1917 at a factory in Madeburg, Germany,' he muttered.

Turning it over she noticed the engravings. She recognised them as Egyptian hieroglyphics. 'Where did you find it?'

'Bid for it at an auction, not many others showed an interest in it so I got it cheaply. Sorry, no idea about its origins', he replied. She was immediately attracted to it and decided she wanted it. After some stiff haggling she put it in her bag and wandered home.

The next day she placed it on the bench in the kitchen when her friend Alison arrived for a chat over a cup of coffee. They were both from Australia so it was comforting to catch up now and again. As the pungent smell of coffee filled the air they chatted 'what's that?' Alison inquired.

'I think it is an artillery shell from the First World War.' They both began examining it.

'How fascinating, what are you going to do with it?'

'No idea', Katie replied dreamily.

'Needs a bit of a polish', her friend observed.

When Alison left Katie went to the local hardware

store and bought some Brasso. After some time and effort, it was gleaming. She looked around her flat and chose a prominent place to display it. It glinted in the sun and became quite a talking point after a few glasses of red. Many a yarn was spun about how it came to be engraved.

Katie eventually returned to Melbourne. She sold most of her possessions and brought little back with her. One item Katie could not relinquish was the artillery shell she had bought at the jumble sale. Although she didn't realise it, it seemed to have a hold over her. Katie never lost her love of jumble sales and began to collect items to sell. She was going through her cupboards and decided it was time to say goodbye to the artillery shell. She thought to herself, let someone else have the enjoyment she'd had when she first bought it. A dealer at the Camberwell market was making offers for her items. When he saw the artillery shell he immediately mentioned a price. After some haggling, she sold it to him.

Return to Australia from WW2 POW camp

On my return to Australia, I gradually settled into civilian life as the physical and mental wounds healed. Falling in love with a beautiful young girl, I got married and we had two sons. Every Sunday we would go to the Camberwell market and buy antiques and other treasures. One Sunday my grandson was rummaging through a box under the table of a stall when I saw something glinting in the sun. My heart missed a beat as my grandson picked up a brass artillery shell, *my* brass artillery shell. He turned to me and asked, 'what's this Grandad, can we buy it?' I just replied 'sure'.

I looked into the face of the stall-holder. To my horror, I thought I recognised him. Suddenly I was paralysed. He had been the guard at that POW hell hole. Fear gripped me until I heard the voice of my grandson. 'Well?' 'Yes,' I answered in a daze. The memories flooded back as I wandered along. I visualised my mates no longer here. My heart beat faster and I began to shake, fear filled me as I thought about what one human being can do to another. Then disgust took over and the feelings of helplessness and anger returned.

At that moment I decided this would be the last time I would allow these feelings to overcome me. I had to make a decision. Would I forgive and forget, or would I have him arrested? The thought of revenge was tempting, but I decided the future was more important than the past. On our return home, my wife got out the Brasso and polished the shell till it shone. She used it for a vase. I never did find out how it had made its way to Australia; nor did I tell my family of the horrors of war that it held for me, and how it had helped me through those terrible days. I never went to the Camberwell market again and wished that all people in the world could live in peace.

Kicking and Screaming to Heaven

Sung-Ju Suya Lee

'Wake up, genius.'[10]

'Repeater.'

'Her, again?!'

'It's the third time this month.'

'Ha, we're only half way.'

'Shit, she's dropping!' A flat line blares on the portable heart monitor. The nurses and paramedics race down the hallway towards the ER. I never feel my limp body banging against the cold guard rails of the stretcher.

[10] First line from *Finders Keepers,* Stephen King

~

Bloody hell. A phone dialing over the loudspeaker pierces my eardrums. Where am I? I open my eyes, but the fluorescent lights blind me. Not here, again! Who's the idiot waking up all the patients in the middle of the night? Damn those nurses.

What's that smell? I lift my arms to cover my nose—these bat wings that are covered with dried blood, hardening over the needle scabs on top of the bruises, and the collapsed vein highway tracks from my finger to my armpit. A bent tube protrudes from my hand, yet I do not feel a thing. I look up and there are two sacks, one clear and one red. I don't even remember my blood type. This thing called life isn't what it's cracked up to be. One day, I am going to beat Einstein (or, did he say God?) at tossing the *dice*. I never mean to kill myself, but often I forget to measure the white powder or take the needle out of my arm. Sheez, I don't have a CrackBerry to remind me of my to-do list.

'Stop it, stop taking my pants.' I can barely hear myself grunt.

The nurses hover over me as they grab and shove me around. They knock over my mobile phone. I see it shatter. My heart breaks since it has the only number to my escape from this hell life. They step on the sim card. I hear it crack. My dealer won't recognise a new number. The nurses pick up the phone pieces, but don't assemble it back together.

'Has anybody called her children, yet?'

‘They didn’t bother coming last time.’

‘Something like they couldn’t get a babysitter at 2am.’

‘The church shelter said they’d drop by, again.’

‘Too bad they can’t tie her to their beds every night.’

Damn, gotta get out of here before my kids kill me... if the nurses call them to get me, again. Whoever that goodie two-shoes was who called the paramedics on me... well, stop doing that. Let me be.

Another night, another chance at survival. If you've never been in an emergency holding area in a downtown city hospital before, well, let me tell you, it’s quite the trip. That eight million and one stories in the naked city ends here, not the jailhouse. If you’re in the morgue, your *story* has been replaced by another sucking air for the first time in another part of this place. These folks here have been kicked out of the good-life coop and most will never see the light at the end of the tunnel. I fit nicely in that category. I stopped minding my own business when I first hit the bottle after he left me and the kids. The nurses here look like Nurse Ratched... too many lives without love. I can hear this hospital is in full swing. Heck, I can smell them all. Please do not throw up... I never want to be like *those* people, stinking up with that mix of vomit, piss and garage grease.

~

I really should stop. Another lie passes through my lips. Gawd, I sound like an addict now. Liars always want more... hmm... more of something that’s missing? Just to fill a void the size of the universe. I see the red button by my finger on the bed, but I don't move.

~

A nurse walks through the side curtain. 'Are you still in pain?'

Pain? No. Why? I can't speak. My mouth feels dry and clamped tight. I just blink at her. She taps a needle and out squirts a clear substance. 'This will help you. It's another shot of morphine. Do you understand?' I blink, again. She injects it into the liquid pipeline attached to my hand. Talk about a tsunami of the mind. Immediately, I never even have a chance to surrender before it hits me. Nor do I even see her leave.

~

The curtains can't keep anything out. Some nurses scuffle into my area as they try to control a woman. Her pants are half-way down.

'They are soaking wet!'

'You've done a number two, lady.'

'No, I don't want to take off my pants!' I hear my own voice screaming at them. I try to speak again, but my tongue is plastered to the back of my throat.

'You can't keep them on.'

'They stink, and you'll get infected.' But the nurses have no impact on this woman. They are angels paying their dues while getting their wings dirty. I do not have my glasses on, but I can see them clearly. What…?

~

'Hey, that old hag, she's got my clothes. I want my clothes

back!' However, it comes out as a grunt. I grunt louder. 'Stop her, she's got my Dr. Who watch on. My kids will be mad as hell if I lose... stop that thief.' Sadly, it is drowned out by the fighting going on. I could always escape with that TV show. That and drugs were my tickets outta here. Not to live in reality is still my only goal.

'No way. Damn you, I'm keeping all of my clothes on!' That woman yells at the nurses. Jeezus, she sounds a lot like me.

The stench becomes overwhelming. 'God damn, lady, take a bath once in your life,' I grunt back.

'Don't take my Dr. Who watch. My kids gave it to me,' that lady screams at the nurses who leave her wristwatch on while finally getting her pants off.

I don't want to mention the nastiness of everyone's language around here. Boy, when did I become such a prude? Nevertheless, I feel a moment of purity which I have never experienced before. Is this what truly devoted people feel? Then bottle it up, sell it to high heaven and get rich. Where do I get the copyright? They continue to ignore me, and even treat me as an inconvenience. This is the story of my life. When did I become invisible? When did destiny close the book on me and leave me behind? I make a mental note to never shoot up ever, again. Don't make this another lie, please. They all hit my bed hard; tossing me almost onto my side. Then, they tumble on to the floor of the next room before I black out.

~

That ringing phone penetrates my skull this time. How can anybody get any rest around here?! Crikey, they better not have called my kids. Where are my clothes? Didn't those nurses get my clothes back from that woman? Which way did they go? I can't feel the floor, though I can control my legs. That's a good sign, I still have free will over my body. I can't tell if it's night or day. There are no windows anywhere. It takes forever for me to even take a small step. It hits me that a fraction of a second counts here more than anywhere else except maybe NASA. It takes all my energy to drag my IV hook-up with me.

~

Oh, right, they went that way to that side of my curtain wall. A family is hovering around an old man... perhaps on his deathbed? He sounds like Morgan Freeman. How many times has he played God on the big screen? A priest is present, but the old man is alive and kicking.

~

'The only thing that matters is my relationship with God,' the old man tells his family.

'Joshua, shhh, keep your strength,' his wife squeezes his hand.

'It's alright, honey. It doesn't matter what I did in my life, good or bad. None of that matters. Only my faith and belief in God.'

But his grandson son looks up from his mobile, 'So,

Grandad, you're saying I can sleep around, drink, steal, kill, whatever… And still get into heaven?'

Joshua nods. His grandson son throws his arms in the air. Touchdown. But, the priest shakes her head. 'Living a clean life is the path…'

~

I walk past, uncertain if I even heard right. Hmmm… What to think? So Hitler, Khan, Saddam, bin Laden, and McVeigh can all go to heaven if they believe in God? Lucifer should have had this information before he defected from that holy place. Hmmm… interesting. I push my IV pole in front of me without any effort now.

There's a funny noise, some gasping and beeping. I pull back the curtain and my heart drops; a young woman in a coma with an airway tube jutting out of her mouth. She is a dead ringer for Sophia Loren. Her head is tilted back and her eyes stare millions of miles beyond this hospital. Sophia Loren manages a smile through the mouth contraption, maybe a good dream or an orgasm? I can't feel my face, so I don't know if I am smiling back at her. I sit on her bed and stroke her hair. Then, she snap turns and stares at me, her eyes pierce right through mine. I jump up and let out a grunt.

'Mistakes are part of the dues one pays for a full life.' WHAT? Her lips never moved; they are glued over the air tube. Yet, her eyes seem lucid. I look up, but the life machine never registers this. Am I hallucinating? What if I caused her to be upset? Who the hell goes up to a stranger and starts stroking their hair? If anybody catches me, they'll think I'm some sort of sicko in the wrong section of the hospital. She starts talking, again, but I can't understand her. I don't know if it's because of the tube or she's speaking another language. Maybe in tongues?

Then suddenly her body stiffens and she arches her back so that she is lying on top of her head. A bright white-golden light streams from the centre of her body. The beeping stops. Her heart line goes flat.

'Code Blue, Bed 4. Code Blue, Bed 4.' The switchboard pages over the loudspeaker. Did I cause this? Little twinkly stars like fairy dust are floating up toward the ceiling. I can almost touch those stars. I lift up my hands and back off. No way, I didn't do anything. A swarm of nurses and doctors surround her as they jostle me aside.

They try to revive her over and over, again. An overwhelming feeling of love and peace come over me. Like nothing I've ever experienced before. Better than when that old hag and nurses busted into my space. My body is a feather.

I shout at the top of my lungs, 'Can't you see the light?' without opening my mouth. Then, they stop and step back.

'Time, 12am.' Sophia Loren's death is noted. The others nod. One types the time in her tablet. One pulls out Sophia Loren's breathing tube. Another pulls the sheet over her face. When people talk about time standing still or some mumbo-jumbo about space and time continuum, this is it. I hope to understand more once I leave this planet.

~

A sharp pain rips through my head. I grab my IV pole, but it slips through my fingers. I hit the floor hard. The lights go out. I dream of ambulance lights twirling around in my head and two old male paramedics lift me up into an ambulance. They are Santa Clauses. Ahhh, wouldn't it be nice if there were two Santas in this world giving all the folks... I am shaken awake by some old scruffy, white-haired male nurses. What's that noise? Is that the fire alarm? … Won't someone answer that damn phone? Don't you just hate it when someone wakes you up from the most exciting part of a dream? As I am taken back to my bed, a little girl stops and smiles at me. I am struck by her angelic face, a cross between Halle Berry and Goldilocks. She waves and holds out a candy for me. I reach out for the candy, but the distance seems to be getting greater the more I stretch out my arm. She looks like my daughter from some decades ago. Her mother walks ahead.

'Hello. Did you come for the *special* candy?' the little girl asks.

'Sweetie, who are you talking to? Come along.' Her mother backtracks and pulls her along. Sweetie resists slightly. I reach for the candy, but then she is out of reach. She tilts her head sideways and waves good-bye. Her mother never makes eye contact with either Sweetie or myself. Was I a good mother? I should treat my kids better next time. Really listen to them, really connect with them once and for all. I'm only kidding myself.

~

Another searing pain blasts through me. Nurses, paramedics and doctors are all running around me now. A sharp electric bolt rushes through my body. My lungs suck in air.

'Clear.' All the nurses sigh with relief. I gasp for more air. I open my eyes. Another nurse stands back with his hands up high holding the defibrillator. I look at the clock on the wall. It reads 12 o'clock. What did I hear before? I can't tell if it's am or pm.

'Can you hear me?' asks a nurse. I stare back and blink.

'Cancel Code Blue, Bed 2. Cancel Code Blue, Bed 2.' The switchboard relays over the loudspeaker.

'You're lucky to be alive.'

'We lost you for a minute.'

'She's stabilised now.'

'Take some blood tests.' Everyone is talking all at once, but the words seem to be bouncing off the walls. Are they talking to me?

One of the nurses leaves the room. The curtain remains ajar so I can see all the action passing by. Man, it is busy tonight. It looks like a shopping mall. People carrying flowers, gifts, books, magazines, suitcases, and fast food. It's too much stimulation. As I close my eyes, I hear something similar I just heard before.

~

'Hello. Want a candy?' A little girl's voice rings out. *What the…?*

I turn my head and see Sweetie standing there with her hand stretched out holding some candy. But, nobody is there. Who is she talking to? 'Sweetie, I'm over here in bed 2.' I try to speak, but the nurses are still poking and prodding me. *'You can give me the candy over here,'* I yell out to her. Yet, my own garble sounds frightened even me. I reach for her.

'Did you say something?' asks one of the nurses as she tucks my limp, dangling arm back on the bed. She looks me right in the eye. She leans in close and adjusts the air tube deeper into my throat. Do I look that scary when I talk to people real close? 'Do you want anything?' I mean to nod, but I barely shake my head. *I want special candy to escape this life.*

'Sweetie, who are you talking to? Come along.' Her mother comes back and pulls her along. Sweetie resists slightly. She tilts her head sideways and waves good-bye. She turns around, and she visibly has Down Syndrome. I don't understand. Didn't she look like my daughter before?

I was right there, she was talking to me, I was reaching out for that candy. *Come back, Sweetie.* I open my mouth to scream, but the air tube just goes in deeper. Where do I press the delete button to get out of this *Twilight Zone*? Or, do I mean Dr. Who's telephone booth? Can I actually be in two places at once? This is not a dream, so it must be déjà vu. Right? I close my eyes to escape this confusion.

~

The phone rings louder over the speakers. It almost shakes the walls. No one is answering it. There must be a lot of people dying tonight, or they are short staffed. Damn those city budget cuts. My hand feels warm and tingly. Is someone holding my hand? I open my eyes. It is Sophia Loren. She's stroking my hair and staring me right in the eye. Huh? I thought she just died. I look at my heart monitor and it says I'm still kicking and breathing. I feel calm and relaxed when she smiles at me.

'Code Blue, Bed 4.' Sophia Loren is surrounded by that same white-yellow fairy dust, as before as the tiny stars take her to heaven. She keeps staring at me till she disappears beyond the ceiling. *Don't go. Come back.* Everything is happening faster than the speed of light. I do not want to blink anymore. I seem to miss things if I do.

When she finally disappears, I am left empty and drained. The kids on the other side of me are hitting the curtain with Joshua's IV line. I hear bits and pieces of their conversation. 'So, Grandad, you're saying I can sleep around, drink, steal, kill, whatever… And still get into heaven?' Déjà vu? Stunned, I don't know what to make of this. It is what it is. I am no longer afraid of what's next. Except, why is it all happening backwards?

~

My mobile phone rings. What's that strange ringtone?

What if it's my kids calling on a different phone? Gotta get it. Wait... I have heard this ring before... here at the hospital.

The broken mobile phone glows on top of my clothes on the chair. Thank gawd, those nurses got my stuff back. I reach for my phone with the cracked screen as the battery hits the floor. The Dr. Who watch on my wrist ticks louder than before. However, I can't get to my mobile in time. Damn, I'll have to do call back. I hope it wasn't a private number. I hate missing calls. Then, the mobile's call answer clicks on automatically by itself and I hear a voice on the other end while still lying in my bed. It's a voice I don't recognise, yet I have known forever. I am filled with purity. It's not the florescent lights I see anymore.

'Wake up, genius.'

Was it God who just helped me pick up my broken mobile phone? I do not have to throw the dice anymore.

A Reconciliation Myth

Bala Mudaly

"Everyone agreed that the day was just right for the picnic at Hanging Rock",[11] wrote the teacher on the board.

'Now who can guess where that famous line comes from?' Mr Logan said with an expectant glance around the class. It was once again creative writing hour for year 10 at Mount Macedon High School.

Two hands shot up–one tentative. A few students shuffled and looked away, not wanting to be called upon.

'Well Ron?'

---

[11] First line from *Picnic at Hanging Rock*, Joan Lindsey

'From over there, Mr Logan.' Ron pointed out the window across the hazy, winter landscape. 'Hanging Rock, Sir. Me and my family had a BBQ there on New Year's Day. Mum and Dad bet on horses.'

Muffled giggles disturbed the class like rustling leaves in a passing breeze.

'Quite right. You've reminded us that there's horse racing at Hanging Rock to mark New Year and Australia Day. Class, if you fix your eyes out there through the window, you'll see an outcrop of jagged volcanic rocks. Barely visible in this miserable weather. Has anyone here explored Hanging Rock?'

Keen students called out, 'me, me, Mr Logan.'

'My Mum saw a movie about girls gone missing ages ago at Hanging Rock,' said Nadia above the chatter.

'Fake news, fake news,' Tom said. '*The Weekend Australian* said so last week. My grandpa was telling Dad at dinner about this article he had read, which said the indigenous folks in Mount Macedon were upset by that story. They've launched the *Miranda Must Go* campaign.'

'Yeah,' mumbled Nullah.

'What's that, Nullah? Please speak up.'

'Bin to the Rock with me Auntie Mavis last summer. Read the story board there behind the tourist information office, Mr Logan. All about the picnic and them girls who got lost. Happened fifty years ago. But Auntie says it's a load of bull and the made-up story just messes up the real history.'

'Can you please explain to the class what Hanging

Rock means to the Kulin nation?'

'Well, I dunno much, Sir, except my mob, the Dja Dja Wurrung, called it *Nyannelong*. Long before white people come, it was a place for secret men's business, like initiation ceremonies.

This elicited puzzled and questioning looks, appeals to Mr Logan to rescue the situation, to offer clarity on what was now turning into a touchy matter.

'That's it in a nutshell, class,' said Mr Logan skirting the issue. He explained that Joan Lindsey's 1967 novel *Picnic at Hanging Rock* told of a group of white school girls on a picnic outing in which a couple of them, together with a teacher, go exploring the rocky outcrop and never return. This happened on 14 February 1900, Valentine's Day. The novel was made into a film, which is now considered an Australian classic. A mystery has since formed around the story. Some say it's pure fiction, but others claim it's based on fact.

'But Nullah is also correct. The local Aboriginal people do wish to reclaim Hanging Rock and promote its sacred heritage.'

'What's the assessment task, Mr Logan? You've not told us.'

'Quite correct, Martha. Let me explain. There'll be two parts to the writing project. Firstly, to help you understand the background, we will watch the Hanging Rock film together during our next double English lesson. Note the date in your diary. Then, you will each study a short piece of fiction I will give you and write your impressions of it. Is this clear?'

Total silence.

'No need to sweat on it,' Mr Logan smiled, sensing apprehension in the air. 'You've studied the basics of creative writing in our previous classes. Here's another opportunity to apply your skills.'

Someone from the back said, 'the reading stuff, Mr Logan, is it difficult?'

'Not difficult at all. I've simply made up a different version of what could have happened to Miranda, the main character in the story. I call it *A Reconciliation Myth.* In your feedback, pay particular attention to the ending. Is it appropriate, or should the story have concluded in some other way?'

Nullah put up his hand, and Mr Logan nodded.

'Sir, I don't think we can manage that. I mean find fault with what you write.'

'Not to worry. You'll do well. Just apply what you've learnt and be bold about it.'

~

As promised, Mr Logan produced the following piece of writing for the class to critique:

While everyone was preoccupied, Miranda, always the dreamer, slipped away unnoticed from the picnic spot. She picked her way through a stretch of tall buffalo grass, the colour of wheat. If someone stopped her, she thought, she'd say she was only following the bees and butterflies to the lively creek close by. But the truth was that the moment she left the carriage, she felt driven by a certainty that destiny was close at hand. Hadn't her mysterious Valentine's Day card promised as much? She was dressed in a flowing white long-sleeved dress fringed with lace. Her flaxen hair, modestly plaited, glowed. Miranda looked every bit a rose about to open itself to possibilities.

She followed a narrow path through fern and grass, crossed a shallow creek stepping over stones and headed towards rocky outcrops just visible through the trees. The path became steeper. Up and up went Miranda. She had the feeling she was the only person alive. The sun whirled and whirled from a cloudless sky. The air was heavy with the smell of eucalyptus. She faltered in the heat and dense haze. Her chest heaved. Her mouth was dry as ash. She sat on a fallen log, discarded her boots, peeled off her gloves and stockings and shook her hair loose.

Miranda climbed higher and entered an unfamiliar world—a moonscape of jagged conical outcrops, caves, sudden passageways, deep pits, precarious boulders, columns of rock, and unexpected courtyards. She scrambled onto a rocky platform to see how much further she had to go, certain she'd know when she arrived. A flock of screeching parrots flew past. A little way to her right soared a monolith, dark against the light. This overbearing Rock was pockmarked, fissured and scarred by lichen. As she shielded her eyes and gazed fixedly at the Rock, Miranda believed she saw the gaunt and age-weary face of an old man. Was he the keeper of Hanging Rock? She felt strangely drawn towards it.

It was high noon. The heat was relentless. Every cell in her body cried to be quenched. Indifferent to their plea, Miranda persisted, propelled by a purpose now beyond understanding. It seemed her thoughts, feelings and senses were dissolving and reforming, dissolving and reforming like clouds in urgent flight. Even the world around her was no longer stable or certain. Shadow and light melded with images of landscape—sky and earth, rock and trees, insects and birds. Ah yes, I'm free-floating in a dream-world, she thought.

Miranda felt as if she had been travelling a long while, almost years. But the distance was covered in accelerated time. Even the sun, unhinged from its zenith, had crossed the sky and arrived in the western horizon, resting a little behind the massive rock-face, which now cast deepening shadows across a confined open space. It was almost twilight.

Miranda knew she had arrived in a special and privileged space. Dizzy from exertion and overwhelmed by the moment, she lowered herself onto her knees. She raised her eyes to the monolith but was blinded by light from the setting sun. No sooner had the sun slipped fully behind the Rock than the its scarred and inscrutable face emerged from the gloom, enormous and majestic. Miranda was transfixed. Her heart raced. As she gazed unblinking upon the Rock, it seemed to shift and take life.

A human figure formed. It stepped out. It was a young man, no older than Miranda but much taller. His naked body was sinewy and taut and glistened a chocolate-purple. His face was broad. He was endowed with well-formed teeth, large bright eyes set in deep sockets, a broad nose, and a mop of soot-black hair. He smiled as if pleased to be set free. The face was remarkably similar to a youthful version of the Rock. He took a few tentative steps towards Miranda. For a moment, he stood on one leg, supported at the knee by the sole of the other. The young man made cracking sounds with his clapsticks. Miranda, mesmerised, did not stir. She did not doubt this was a fully grown young man, unashamedly displaying his manhood. But she hadn't seen anyone like him before, not even in picture books. A strange warmth welled up in her, consuming her heart and mind. Her cheeks burned. It was altogether a strange new feeling. She felt an urge to rise and touch him.

The young man circled her a few times, studying Miranda. Suddenly he jumped back and uttered excited sounds in a strange tongue. He leaned into Miranda's face and fired rapid questions, pointing to her breasts. She froze. The next moment, he threw down his clapsticks and ran off.

The light was fading fast. The air was cooler now, more bearable. A pale moon was becoming brighter. Miranda was intoxicated with weariness and wonder. She fell back on her haunches and closed her eyes.

A rustling sound disturbed her. The young man had returned looking very different. White clay covered his face, except for circles exposing his eyes, mouth and nose. Horizontal stripes of yellow and red ochre crossed his chest and upper arms and white dots ran down his lower arms. He assumed a crouching posture with his hands up at the elbows, each clutching a sprig of speckled yellow-white flowers. His eyes, deceptively larger than before, danced from side to side. Still crouching, he stomped in deliberate steps towards Miranda and back, then side to side, and every now and then circled her—as if he was imitating the courtship dance of a lyrebird. It was hypnotic. Miranda soon found her consciousness drifting into a cloud.

Darkness gave way to the yellow light of dawn. The Rock glistened with dew. Stillness prevailed. Her purpose spent, Miranda sat propped up at its base, bare feet stretched out in front. From a little distance, it seemed as if she was fast asleep, folded in the embrace of the monolith's deep shadow. Strands of her tangled locks fluttered now and again, as a gentle breeze passed by. Her hands rested on her lap, lightly touching two wilting sprigs of speckled yellow-white flowers. A mottled butterfly flitting uncertainly in the air hovered for a moment over the flowers only to be scared off by a pair of curious honey-eaters, which landed at Miranda's feet. They chirped and hopped about looking for feed, even pecking at the flowers on her lap. A monitor lizard emerged from the shadow and lifted his head to sunlight but scurried away when he sensed an approaching threat.

Miranda did not hear the urgent calling of her name 'Miraaanda, Miraaanda' from the picnic grounds far below, nor the yelping of dogs. Her face, soiled and sunburnt from relentless heat and exertion, was serene. The sounds of men and dogs echoed and echoed, only to be lost in the empty spaces and crevices all around.

~

Mr Logan was impressed with his students' varied responses and complimented them unreservedly. There was a spontaneous ripple of nods and smiles.

'I couldn't tell if Miranda lived or died,' said Bruno at the back of class.

'Of course, she died, silly,' said Sylvia. 'That's why she didn't hear the search party calling her. And why else would birds hop all over her without fear?'

Now that Sylvia has settled that matter,' said Mr Logan, 'let's discuss your comments on how I ended my version of the story. It interests me that hardly anyone seemed happy with it. Instead, you've come up with contrasting and original ideas. Let's get some representative examples.'

With this Mr Logan called on three students to speak their mind in front of the class based on their written comments.

Martha said the ending upset her. 'Miranda was a foolish girl. She took off on her own without water and a hat. Got into strife and lost her mind. She should have known the summer heat was a killer. I'd have felt so much better if the search party had found her dying but still managed to save her.'

'Yeah, yeah,' shouted a few students in unison. Others clapped.

Mr Logan thanked Martha for her confidence. 'Now, Nullah, you think otherwise, don't you?'

Nullah's shoulders slumped. 'Can I just read what I've written rather than talk, Mr Logan?'

'Certainly, but from next to me, facing the class, so your voice carries.'

'I know why Miranda got into strife, Mr Logan. She shouldn't have gone to that place. And not taken up with that young blackfella.' Nullah raised his head, gazed in the direction of the window where the sun shone from a clear sky. 'But I also feel sorry it happened this way.' With that he hastened to his seat.

Except for some paper shuffling and a cough or two, there was silence. Those closest to the window looked out. Dark and craggy outcrops stood out over a canopy of stringy-bark and blackwood trees.

'We've listened to two divergent views,' said Mr Logan. 'But a small but significant number of you suggested an ending you considered more satisfying. Nadia reflects this third view.'

Nadia sauntered to the front, tossing her dark plaits behind her. The boys clapped and cheered until they were scolded.

'Well, we all know about Valentine's Day and all that stuff,' said Nadia. 'I think Miranda went out looking for her perfect boyfriend, and somehow got carried away.' This comment raised snide remarks, whispers and cat-calls. Nadia stopped and gave the class her middle finger.

'Come now, quieten down and listen respectfully. Give Nadia a chance to finish. And Nadia, what you just did was rude and quite unnecessary.'

'I think Miranda found who she was looking for. The black guy who danced before her, all made up. I think true love is everything. It should be a winner every time.'

'But what about the ending, Nadia? What's your suggestion?'

'Sir, the best thing that could happen is for the two to escape deep in the night, escape from Hanging Rock into the valley below. Come morning, we see the two walking, hand in hand, over the open grassland, making for the nearest waterhole where they find an Aboriginal camp. They make their home there and enjoy good times.'

The students erupted into a wave of cheering and clapping, confirming the prevailing sentiment of the class. Unnoticed at the rear of the room, Nullah remained still, his hands resting quietly on the desk in front of him.

The Coat Hanger

Robert New

'Art theft, of course,' said the elegant man, 'has been overdone. By now it's thoroughly boring.'[12]

'That's not an answer. Let me confirm I have this right,' Jimmy "Mug" Punter said to his new acquaintance, Bucky Fuller. 'You want me to break into a dry cleaner to steal an item of clothing.'

Mug was in his usual booth in Bacchus Bar at the unusual time of midday. Bucky had appeared by appointment a short while after he'd arrived. The chair at

[12]First line from 'Ask a Silly Question', *Thieves Dozen*, Donald E Westlake

the top end of the booth was too small for Bucky's size. He shifted uncomfortably and glared at Mug like he was a child.

'Yes,' said Bucky, taking a breath and letting his weight drive the air from his lungs. Mug was uncertain his response wasn't just a sonically blessed wheeze.

Mug raised an eyebrow. 'One item?'

'Yes,' Bucky wheezed again.

'What piece of clothing could be worth you paying me forty thousand to steal for you?'

'Don't want the clothing, just the coat hanger.'

Mug rolled his eyes.

'Just the coat hanger? Look, far be it for me to refuse a payday, but I'm happy to get you a coat hanger for much less than that. It would be real nice too—wood inlay and gold hook and stuff.'

Bucky sighed. 'You mean *really* nice.'

'Whatever. What's so special about this coat hanger?'

'It contains the key to the secret of success. Look, just get it. You can keep what's on it.'

Mug shook his head. 'It's your money.'

'Time's important. Can you do it tonight?'

'No. There's no way I can plan and execute an operation that quickly.'

'I'll give you an extra five thousand.'

'No.' Mug's voice wavered. 'It can't be done.' He really shouldn't let himself be tempted.

'Extra ten, or I'll get someone else.'

'Okay, I'll do it,' Mug said. 'What was the item

number again?'

'Two, seven, three, one.' Mug dutifully wrote the number down.

'I muddle numbers sometimes. Can you confirm I've written this correctly?'

Bucky nodded, reached into his jacket pocket and passed over a crumpled business card. 'This is the address.'

'Okay, okay. I've got it,' said Mug.

~

Mug assembled his crew; Slavish was his gadget and safe-cracking guy and Murky was his driver and lookout. An hour later, they were with him at Bacchus Bar.

'Guys, we have a job,' Mug said.

'Oh yeah?' said Murky.

'Yeah, some guy wants us to break into a dry cleaner and steal a coat hanger.' He tried to remain deadpan, but a smile still escaped onto his face.

'What?' Murky and Slavish said in unison.

'Yep. Fifty grand between us to steal a coat hanger.'

'Awesome,' said Murky.

'No way. Why on earth?' said Slavish. 'Wait. Are you having a lend?'

'Nope. Fifty thousand to steal a coat hanger.' Mug smiled. Their reaction had been perfect.

'The best bit is they're a *dry cleaner*. I mean who steals from a dry cleaner? So pretty simple security.'

'Awesome,' said Murky again.

'What's the catch?' asked Slavish.

'Who says there's a catch?' said Mug.

'C'mon Mug, for someone to pay that much for so little, there must be a catch.'

'Well, umm… the job has to be done tonight.'

Slavish stood and reached to shake Mug's hand. 'Thanks for the drink Mug. See you on Saturday.'

'Sit down Slavish. It's not impossible.'

'But it sounds like a setup.'

'It's not. The guy passed the usual checks.'

'Yeah, but what's the rush.'

'He wants to get it before someone else collects the item tomorrow.'

'I'll humour you. What are the details?'

'The dry cleaner is on Oxford Street and we're after item…' Mug checked his bit of paper, 'two, seven, three, one.'

'Mmmm.' Slavish nodded. 'What else?'

Mug shrugged. 'That's all I know.'

'No details on security, no entry or exit plan and no means of concealing the item if we get caught.'

'Yep,' said Mug.

'No plan then, just wing it?' said Slavish.

'It worked for us on that job Murky brought us last year.'

'Which you hated,' Murky said. 'You were pissed we had to abandon your plan.'

'Yeah, well maybe I learnt we could do things more simply.'

'Or you just want the money,' Murky suggested.

Mug smiled. 'Maybe. It's a simple job though, and no need to fence anything.'

'True. A simple payday could be good. I'm in,' said Slavish.

'Me too,' said Murky.

~

The dry cleaner was in the middle of a long row of shops. It had a carpark at the back, where Mug, Murky and Slavish were huddled in Murky's nondescript brown van. Murky had placed a sign on the sides of the van reading "James's Drycleaning," the name of the business they were about to break into. It wasn't a good sign as it was just painted on a magnetic whiteboard, but they all agreed it was better than nothing.

'How long do you want to be in there for?' asked Murky.

'No more than sixty seconds. We should just be in and out. I mean all we have to do is go in, find one item and leave.'

'No way you'll be in and out in that time,' said Murky.

'Oh yeah, wanna bet?' asked Mug.

'What's my share?'

'Just under seventeen thousand,' replied Mug.

'Three thousand says you won't be outside in ninety.'

'You're on.'

'I'll take a hundred secs,' said Slavish.

'What are we saying?' asked Murky.

'Let's make it fifteen grand each and bonus five to the person whose time is closest,' suggested Mug.

'Done,' the others replied in unison.

'Starting from when the shop door is open to when you've got the item and have left the building,' said Murky.

'Of course.' Mug looked at Slavish. 'And no going slow just to win.'

'Thieves' honour.' Slavish grinned, 'Who's timing?'

'Me,' said Murky. 'I'll keep you informed over coms.'

Mug and Slavish put on their hoodies and fake glasses and got out of the van. They grinned when they saw the door had electronic locks. Slavish found the external fuse box, picked the padlock on it and quickly shut the power to the block of shops. A few metres away they could see the dry cleaner's door release and open a couple of centimetres.

~

Mug and Slavish entered the dry cleaners. Along the side wall was a narrow bench with a sewing machine. The rest of the store was filled by a suspended, mechanised track which twisted and turned so it occupied most of the space. Hanging from the track's rack were what looked like a thousand items of clothing inside plastic bags. Mug and Slavish glanced at each other and shrugged. There was no order to the numbers on the tags. The track was designed to bring the required item to the front when it's number was typed into a keypad by the front counter. The tags were scanned as they passed the collection point.

'Twenty seconds,' said Murky into their ears.

They soon found where to turn the track on, but then

realised that by cutting the power it wouldn't work.

'I didn't bring the gear to power this ourselves. It would take too long to set up anyway. Plus, they'd know we'd been here if the rack moved,' said Slavish.

'Fine. We'll just have to look for it ourselves.' They began scanning the tags.

'What was the number again?'

'Two, seven, three, one.'

'Nope, this was two, one, three, seven.'

'Forty seconds,' said Murky. Mug and Slavish tried to speed up their searching.

'This is ridiculous. It's almost the proverbial needle,' said Slavish.

'Yep.'

'One minute,' said Murky, his voice rising in excitement.

'Dammit. I'm out,' said Mug unhappily.

'Seventy seconds,' said Murky.

Mug kept reading the numbers. 'Got it,' he said as he grabbed an item and raced for the exit.

'Eighty-nine seconds. Looks like I win!' Murky said, unable to keep the grin out of his voice. Mug and Slavish scowled. In the back of the van, they looked at the dress on the coat hanger.

'Slavish, you can have the dress for your girl. Looks like it would suit her,' Murky said with false magnanimity.

The dress was bright red and cut to be revealing. Slavish's frown turned briefly to a smile. He was probably picturing his girlfriend in the dress.

Fifteen minutes later, they were back in Bacchus Bar and had ordered a round of celebratory drinks. Mug phoned Bucky to say they had the item he was after and were in the bar waiting for him.

~

Bucky blocked the light from the doorway as he entered. He walked with some effort over to the bar and spoke briefly to the Rick the bartender, before joining them at the booth. He placed a briefcase on the table.

'Where is it?'

Mug handed over the coat hanger, with the item tag still attached.

Bucky turned red. 'Is this a joke?'

'What do you mean?'

'I wanted item two, seven, three, one, not one, three.' Bucky looked like he was about to explode. He put his hand on his heart as though he was having a heart attack.

'Dammit Mug, you know you're meant to check with us when your dyslexia could be an issue,' said Slavish.

'There wasn't time,' Mug said apologetically. Thanks to the damn bet.

'I'm sorry for the mistake. If you don't mind waiting, I know it's nearly midnight, but the bar doesn't close until two. We'll be back within thirty minutes,' Mug said as politely as he could. He looked guiltily at Slavish and Murky.

Bucky signalled to Rick to cancel his order as the others ran from the bar.

~

Mug and Slavish approached the back door of the dry cleaner. In their rush, they hadn't noticed a policeman in the shadows who emerged and approached them.

'Hello Gents. There was a report of some unusual activity earlier this evening. I'm afraid you'll have to come back tomorrow.'

Over the in-ear coms, Mug heard the sound of Murky getting out of the car to remove the magnetic signs on the van.

'But they advertise twenty-four-hour pick up,' Slavish moaned. Mug just managed to stifle a laugh.

'The door's open, but it seems like the power is off. I'll get it for you. What's the number?'

'Two, seven, three, one,' they said in unison.

'Okay. You wait here.'

A minute later the policeman returned and handed a dry-cleaning bag to Mug. Mug took it and hoped he concealed his disbelief by saying, 'Thank you.'

They walked as normally as they could manage to the van, grateful they'd parked around the corner from the store. All three double-checked the number. Only then did Mug and Slavish burst out laughing.

Slavish continued to grin after the others stopped.

'What's up with you?' asked Mug.

'Don't you see I won,' he said triumphantly.

'Won what?'

'The bet. It took well over 100 seconds to retrieve the item, so I win.'

'Nup,' said Murky, 'I won fair and square.'

They both looked to Mug.

'The bet was how long it would take to get the coat hanger and get out. You added that bit Murky.'

'So?'

'We didn't get the right one until now. And that's about a few thousand seconds. One hundred is nearest to that.'

Murky appeared crestfallen. 'Dammit.'

Mug laughed, while Slavish grinned even more broadly.

'Don't worry Murky, this time you can keep the clothing.' They all looked at the dark blue suit. It would probably suit Murky. Maybe he'd wear it to his court appearance in a few weeks.

~

As they re-entered Bacchus Bar, Bucky signalled to Rick, who nodded in response. The group sat in their booth. Mug was surprised Bucky hadn't tried to take their seats, but then he realised Bucky wouldn't fit in the booth. The briefcase was still on the table. Mug gave him the coat hanger.

Bucky smiled and started unwinding the coat hanger with a pair of pliers he'd produced from his jacket pocket. Rick brought over a large bowl of steaming water he held with oven mitts, and then fetched a glass of cold water.

Mug and Murky looked confused. Slavish smiled. 'Oh wow,' he said.

'What?' asked Mug and Murky in unison.

'Is the wire nitinol?' asked Slavish, his eyes widening.

'Yes, how'd you know about that?' asked Bucky, without looking up from trying to untangle the wire.

'I did most of a mech eng degree a few years ago.'

'Mmm,' Bucky's replied was barely a grunt, nevertheless the surprise showed on his face.

Slavish spoke enthusiastically. 'Nitinol is what they call a shape memory alloy. It's a special blend of metals that has a crude form of memory. Basically, you form it into a shape at high temperature, cool it and then you can make it into any shape you want. When you heat it again it'll return to the shape you set at the high temperature.'

'Wait. You're trying to tell me a piece of metal can have a memory,' asked Mug.

'Yes.'

'You're nuts,' said Murky.

'Not according to my doctor,' Slavish said with a grin. 'Just watch.'

Bucky finished unravelling the coat hanger. He lowered it into the bowl of near boiling water. Murky and Mug gasped as the metal began twisting by itself. It transformed until it had formed a new shape which looked like a series of numbers.

‘Cool isn’t it?’ said Slavish. ‘You know, I’ve never thought of using it to conceal a code, but it’s actually a pretty awesome idea. I mean you could make it into anything and no one would know you were hiding something. It could be the spring in a ballpoint pen, the underwire on a bra, part of a suitcase…’ Slavish trailed off as he started thinking of the possibilities.

‘Thank you,’ Bucky wheezed as he handed over a bulging envelope. ‘It’s got uses. Now stop talking and let me…’

The group fell silent as Bucky entered the code into the electronically controlled briefcase. It gave a satisfying click as it unlocked. Bucky opened the case to reveal a bottle of Scotch and a sheet of paper.

‘This, gentlemen, is one of the finest whiskies in the world, but it’s not the most valuable thing here. On that sheet of paper is the secret of success. I had someone else steal the case for me yesterday. Their owner will have discovered this by now and will suspect me as I recently drafted his will and made a lot of comments about wanting to know what was written on here.’

Bucky pointed to the paper. ‘I couldn’t believe he was going to leave it to his son, who would probably mix the whisky with cola, and not appreciate the wisdom.’

Bucky shuddered, his huge frame taking a while to settle again. He reached for his heart once more and then took a sip of water.

He picked up the piece of paper and began reading silently.

~

The secret of success comes from accepting a facet of human nature; the average person feels losses twice as much as gains. This leads to a loss aversion— a hesitancy to accept risk even when the odds are in your favour. Most people, when confronted with a fifty-fifty bet would baulk at wagering if they were risking as much as they could gain. So, if offered a chance to win or lose ten dollars on the result of a coin toss, the average person would say no or might try once and then stop due to the fear of losing money. Regardless, the smart man wouldn't take this bet repeatedly. However, if you altered the odds so they were in your favour such as you only risking $4 to win $6 on a coin toss, then over repeated trials you'd make a significant amount of money. However, due to loss aversion many still wouldn't take this bet as they're too afraid of losing. The trick to turning this understanding into long-term success is to realise it's not about gambling at all. It's about not viewing each opportunity in your life as a unique event. It's about understanding how life is a series of little moments, little chances where accepting a moderate amount of risk could lead to reward. Sure, you'll lose some of the time, but over multiple opportunities, on aggregate, you'll come out ahead. So publish that story, invest in that start-up, tell that person how you really feel. Take *all* the opportunities you can which are slightly more likely to work out, than not. That is the secret of success.

~

Bucky smiled and put the paper into his pocket without saying what was on it. 'I have to say hiding the code for the briefcase was ingenious, but a smart person wouldn't have revealed all the details in a single document, even if it was their will.'

Bucky continued to talk as he closed the briefcase, his voice no longer directed at anyone in particular.

'I'll most likely be dead tomorrow, either because my client has killed me or my heart has given out—the doctor has given me two weeks. Once I've passed that paper on to my son, I'll crack the whisky and I can die a happy man. Goodbye gentlemen.'

Bucky stood and walked unsteadily out of the bar, taking the briefcase with him. In a state of shock, Mug silently divided the money from the envelope. He looked at the twisted coat hanger on the table and sighed. Murky and Slavish nodded.

'Thanks Mug that's one for the grandkids,' said Murky.

'Here, you may as well have this too,' said Mug as he handed the wire to Slavish.

'Thirty grand, a magic wire, a dress for my girl, and a tale to tell,' Slavish said. 'Best night in ages!'

Tangle

Andy Russell

All this happened, more or less[13]. I'm sure that you'll excuse any small lapses of memory given the things I went through. Anyway, here's what took place as best as I can remember. When the head-splitting buzz stopped I found that I could think again. Even so, everything felt strange. Everything looked unfamiliar. I could see the whole room, including things behind me. *Weird, it's a bit like having eyes in the back of your head,* I thought. There were limits though. Try as I might I couldn't move my eyes. After some trial and error, I managed to get a view of the

[13] First line from *Slaughterhouse Five,* Kurt Vonnegut

floor by tilting my head sideways. There were a number of things scattered around, but none that I recognised. Even so, one seemed significant. It reminded me of food … of companionship … of conversation. As I puzzled over this, I felt a prickling sensation spreading up the back of my neck. The past was all becoming clearer now and pulling into focus.

'Bring us another beer, would ya?' There was no reply. I wiped my mouth with the back of my hand and drew a deep breath. Then I remembered.

'Just popping out for more beer luv,' Chantelle had called out before the front door slammed. I looked down at the empty beer cans, and then back to the dusty insides of the television set. There was nothing for it, I would have to get on and repair the TV. With any luck, I might be able to catch the last half hour of the match.

'Polly wants a cracker. Polly wants a big cracker!' I turned and gave the bird a mock frown.

'Shut your beak, you stupid cocky,' I was not being serious. Inherited from my father, the sulphur-crested cockatoo was my oldest and probably my best friend. Reluctantly, I turned my attention back to the TV set. There seemed to be nothing wrong with it, at least nothing that was obvious to a motorcycle mechanic. Acting on a sudden inspiration, I plugged in the set and watched intently, unsure of what I was looking for. A tiny purple spark fizzed between one of the thicker wires and the metal chassis.

'Gotcha,' I whispered and reached in to move the

wire. A loud buzzing noise seemed to fill my head. Electric current contracted the muscles in my hand and arm, freezing them in place. With detached fascination, I was aware that the edges of my field of view were dimming. Blackness spiralled in towards the centre until a single bright spot was all that remained. Finally, that spot too was gone, leaving nothing.

Waves of soft, black velvet washed over my sprawled body. The rhythmic surges loosened my attachment to the warm and still twitching flesh. My disembodied consciousness drifted upwards into the light. From above, I could see the television set upended on the floor and my own twisted body with outstretched hand still locked around the cable. *So this is what it's like to be dead*, I thought, *could be worse.* Then something snagged. The gentle upward motion stopped.

'Have you got the telly fixed yet?' Chantelle called as she banged the front door. At first, she must have thought that I'd succumbed to the six cans of beer and fallen asleep. Her eyes widened as she must have realised what had really happened and her hand stifled an involuntary scream. Fortunately, I saw that Chantelle remembered the handy little fridge magnet provided by the local member of parliament. That told her the number to call.

The ambulance crew were calm and efficient. By comparison with most emergencies, electrocution was clean and neat. Disconnect the power, defibrillator, cardio-pulmonary resuscitation, oxygen. In a few minutes, they had finished. Satisfied with their handiwork, they gently rolled my body onto a stretcher. After all the equipment had been removed and the offending TV set banished to the garden shed the room was quiet. Now, although still a bit patchy I could remember most of what had happened.

~

'The hospital's keeping him alive on some sort of machine. But, they say his brain seems to have stopped working.'

'Electrification's not a bad way to go, Chantelle. He probably didn't suffer.' It was Shane, from the house next door. Those were the first civil words I'd heard him speak in the past five years. Shane put his arm around Chantelle's shoulders as she shuddered at the thought of it.

How considerate of Shane, I thought. *Perhaps it was my fault that we never got on.* Shane edged a little closer and let his right hand slide down until it cupped Chantelle's breast. I watched in horrified fascination as Chantelle relaxed against Shane's broad chest and turned to look into his eyes. Quickly, I selected a mixture of invective and profanity that would express my outrage. But, when it came out what I heard myself say was:

'Who's a pretty boy then?' The stunned silence that followed was finally broken by Chantelle.

'It's ok Shane. That's just Gavin's parrot.' However, under the baleful gaze of the bird, they seemed to find it difficult to recapture their previous intimacy. Eventually,

Chantelle pulled Shane to his feet and led him from the room. In the silence that followed, I became aware that I'd developed an irresistible craving for birdseed.

~

'Into the cage you pea-brained parrot. We're going for a ride.' It was Chantelle holding up the wire birdcage. I didn't care much for Chantelle's tone of voice, but then I had been chained to a perch for the past two weeks. It would be good to get outside for a while. I only had a few moments to enjoy the unfamiliar feeling of a breeze ruffling my feathers before Chantelle juggled the cage into the back of Shane's car.

'The doctor at the hospital says there's been no improvement.' Chantelle steadied the cage with one hand and lent forwards so that Shane could hear her from the back seat. 'They're going to unplug the machine tonight and let him go.'

I was enjoying the change of scenery, the streets, the cars, and the people. For some reason, it didn't disturb me that it was my body that Chantelle was talking about.

The clinic was clean and bright and smelt of dogs and disinfectant. I guessed that Chantelle had booked an appointment because we were immediately ushered into an examination room by a veterinary nurse.

'The vet will be along shortly. Perhaps you can tell me what the problem is?' Chantelle turned to the nurse and began what appeared to me to be a carefully prepared story.

'His owner died two weeks ago and he's pining away.

He won't eat. We don't want to see him suffer.' I sensed the nurse tense as she worked out where the story was leading. 'It would be a kindness to put him down.'

The nurse must have decided that this cockatoo was docile because she opened the cage door and let me hop onto her outstretched wrist. Was it the touch of her hand … the sound of her voice … her eyes … her scent? Whatever it was I felt as though I was being electrocuted for a second time. It was amazing that such strong emotions could be triggered quite casually and without obvious cause. Sure, she was attractive and had the most captivating eyes, but there was definitely something more.

'I'm sure that the vet will see that your cockatoo is in excellent health.' The nurse appeared to be choosing her words carefully. 'There is no way that she would consider putting it down. If you really don't want to keep it then I'm sure we could find a good home.'

This was followed by a stony silence broken by the receptionist who came bursting into the room.

'Could you come quickly?' she addressed the nurse in an urgent tone. 'A wallaby has been injured in a car accident. The vet needs your help in the other examination room.' The nurse returned me to my cage.

'Wait here until I come back with the vet,' she insisted. As soon as we were alone, Chantelle took charge of the situation.

'Come on Shane, pick up the cage, and let's get out of here before that nurse comes back. It's obvious they won't do it. You should've wrung the parrot's neck like I asked you to.'

~

With Chantelle giving directions, we drove to a point where the road ran beside a reservoir.

'You wait in the car, Shane. If this is going to get done, I can see I'll have to do it myself.' From the parapet, I felt the cage fall straight down into a deep part of the reservoir. The open wire mesh cage sank instantly pulling me down with it. I tried to hold my breath, but the shock of the cold water knocked the wind out of me. I was getting dizzy … starting to black out. I struggled and beat my wings and ... and struggled and beat my arms. Echoing voices sounded far away. A sharp pain in my arm, and then all was quiet.

~

Chantelle was clearly surprised when she saw how much I'd improved. I was propped up in bed, and no longer had the ventilator tube taped to my mouth. But I was still hooked up to all sorts of drips and monitoring machines.

'The doctor was sure you wouldn't recover.' I nodded. There was a long pause. 'They were very surprised when you came round last night.' I nodded again. I could see that this wasn't getting any easier. Chantelle must have realised that she had to get straight to the point. She took a deep breath. 'Gavin, I'm leaving you. Shane n' me are moving up to Queensland.' I started to nod again but Chantelle kept on talking. 'I'll take my things and leave the key with the landlord.'

'Yes, sure, take anything you want,' I replied. Chantelle seemed to be surprised. She must have come psyched up for an argument and was knocked off balance by what she saw as my meek agreement. Under her breath, she whispered. 'Perhaps, there's some sort of brain damage after all?'

Just as Chantelle made a move to leave, I asked the crucial question.

'There is one thing I'd like to know.'

'What's that, Gavin?'

'Which veterinary clinic was it?' Chantelle pretended that she didn't understand. I gave her a prompt. 'You know, the clinic where you took my cockatoo.' She gave me a strange look. I could see that she must have thought that I couldn't possibly know about the clinic. It looked as though her one thought was to get away as soon as possible. She rummaged in her shoulder bag and came up with a battered card advertising the veterinary clinic. My last glimpse of her was through the wired glass of the swing doors. I turned over the card in my hand. I felt sure that the nurse had liked me as a cockatoo. Would she also be attracted to me as a human being? I had to find out.

A Portrayal of Defeat, and Hope

Robert Sayegh

'Attention', a voice began to call[14], but the young man's eyes glazed east and up to the hill; the sun was about to set behind him beyond the open sea. His athletic body stood commanding, muscles stiff and solid, like an invincible armour, breathing slowly around his failed soul.

'Careful', another voice called as a thin old lady continued to ride her bicycle loaded with a full basket of bread. Maybe she threw a curse, but the wind did not carry it to his ears.

'Why?' is probably a better call, thought the young

---

[14] First line from *Island*, Aldus Huxley

man as the question had been rhyming in his mind for long moments now. But that question is undeniably the mark of his soul's defeat, retreat, un-conceit. It merely means, one ceased trying.

How many beginnings and how many ends must a man go through before giving from within? But the question did not pass into his consciousness, as it was already answered and settled dead in his heart. A human heart now crumbled and shrunk to just beat, and sustain the man's life, naked from his dreams, stripped from his aspirations within the bigger world around.

The street was busy, noises filled the air, but to the young man it was all like a veil of dust. None of it was relevant or required any attention. One would imagine that if a victory is followed by celebration and energetic happy cheering, that a defeat would follow with utter silence. Yet defeat is not a mourning; life, after all, has not ended for those who remain. Life appears to continue as usual with open shops, wandering people, noisy streets as if nothing happened; as if inside every defeated person something else takes place. But that's not the case.

'Watch your step', once again he absently heard a cry and took a step back, still facing away from the community centre's closed gates, unable to watch. More than closed, they were marked by police crime scene tape, banning entrance to the premises. He was anxious that looking at the tape would make him feel dizzy and sick at the bottom of his lungs again. The notorious red tape has become a weakness against his will powers. First it was the folk dancing club, then the weight-lifting gym, and now, helping drug addicts, was added to the list of banned activities for him to do.

Who wants to count all those failed attempts? A champ himself and popular icon within the city walls, all he cared about was serving his community, by teaching and bringing everyone together. 'Keeping the young away from the streets' he kept telling anyone who cared to listen, and now he found himself in the streets again.

What other occupation could be meaningful to him after all? But the Occupation, with its authorities had other plans, such that involved negation and nothingness.

Murmurs from the passers-by occasionally reached his ears. Some saying it was unjust to treat him this way, if only he were from a different 'background'. Others would discard it all insisting the boy is a failure or would scoff saying he should have filled the right papers on time. Maybe it was cruelty, or maybe just miscommunication, but no one seemed able to bridge the gap.

'Why' the question arose again, within. Why one, once feeling power or righteous, would allow themselves such disregard? He heard the threats many time and disregarded them one by one. 'Train soldiers in the military', 'your martial arts skills are useless without pupils', 'you will earn immunity and a decent livelihood'. But he refrained, and openly rejected the offers. Partially because he disdained violence—especially of armies, but mainly to maintain his remaining dignity and not cooperate with the victorious; if defeated then so be it.

The young man took a deep breath, steadied his sight ahead, and dragged his legs hurriedly yet heavily to the other side of the road towards the hill.

The curse of the hill of despair, that's what it is, he thought as he was climbing up. Some call it Napoleon's hill. Some say that the great general built the hill with his army, then settled on that hill for three months and launched eleven futile attacks on the city; which had kept its resilience since the dawn of time. Nuzzled between the sea from west and north, the fearless thousand-years-old walls ran east and south.

Some also say, that after months of siege, Napoleon himself stood one day facing the city walls and the sea, while the sun-blasted his sight from above. Before commanding his defeated soldiers to retreat, he sent a last gesture by letting a cannon shoot his hat into the city, so that at least a part of him would enter its walls.

And here is the young man standing facing this hill, a descendant of those who fought the invader off and stopped him from conquering the world at whim, feeling the burden of dimming his past and future. A conqueror's failure is but temporary, mere delayed victory pending the next endeavour, yet a defender's failure is abrupt and permanent; it erases a whole history and eradicates all possible futures.

As the sun hurried to set, the man kept climbing towards the top of the hill. This was a special day after all. And the hill holds a secret gate to one of the most wonderful scenes possible on earth. Facing the sea in the west and the far dwarfed hills in the east, every lunar month the sight is there for those who care to appreciate when our two celestial marks align at opposite horizons. As the sun begins to set in a spectrum of crimson tingling waters and clouds, the full moon starts to rise and wake into the blue of life over the hazy far tops. Beginning and ending synchronising in space and time.

"Attention!" A voice began to call within…

Snakes Alive!

Brook Tayla

'Years! Years!' [15]

Arna had had the same thought as the alarm went off every morning—for years. She pushed the snooze button and drifted back into a snug dream. When it went off again ten minutes later, she dragged herself straight into the shower and peed down the plughole. When she got out, she pulled a 'blah' face at herself in the mirror.

'Arna Williams, you need a new job—you better get on to that!' she said out loud to herself.

She got dressed, tied up her thick, blonde hair, threw

[15] First Line from a short story written by Eva Hornung

on a bit of make-up and stumbled out the door.

She arrived at the office with the same unnameable dissatisfaction in every part of her being that she had felt every morning for the last few years; a kind of nauseousness. She'd thought this job, journalist at the *Australian News*, was going to be ideal, but it had not gone in the direction she'd envisaged. She thought becoming a journalist meant that people would stand up and listen to what she had to write and be responsive, but they were passive in comparison to her expectations. Journalism hadn't take her down the path of freedom she'd expected either. She was directed from 'above' and told which stories to investigate and follow. Interesting and breaking news articles went to older, longer-standing writers and frustratingly she was left to write the fillers. They were not 'her' stories. She wanted to write 'her' stories.

She turned on her computer and went to get a coffee.

'Hey darling, how's my girl?' It was her slimy editor with his over-inflated ego and sense of entitlement. His daily presence was part of what irritated her and made her lose interest in her job.

'Grrr', she grunted in return. Her rudeness didn't even register with him. At least today he slithered on to someone else without further penetrating her personal space.

'I'll just check my Facebook,' she thought about mid-morning. Scrolling down she saw one of those viral videos. 'Skinned Alive' it read, with a picture of a snake. She hated snakes, feared snakes and never felt compassion towards them in a way she did about other animals, but she clicked on it anyway.

It went no longer than a minute. A man grabbed hold of a live snake. He slit it open straight down the belly with a razor blade, then up and over the back of its head, grabbed hold of an edge and stripped it of its skin in one quick and simple movement. With disdain, he threw it on a pile of other writhing pythons that had been subjected to the same fate. It was the close-up at the end that affected her. This raw, skinless, baby-pink creature had an indescribable fear in its eyes. It was no longer a beady eye of a snake, it was a universal eye, an eye with depth, with meaning, with feeling, with devastation. It barely moved—a sole tear escaped its eye.

She replayed it and replayed it again. Her stomach turned, her negative views of humanity reconfirmed. That tiny pink face could have been any creature, skinned back to primordial existence. Her devastation made it too painful to cry but down her right cheek Arna also shed a solitary tear—hot, burning and acidic.

~

Her mission began. She would expose those bastards and do something about it. That snake had ignited a flame within her, that for too long, had been just flickering. She would be the poison that would bite back and wipe out the snakeskin industry and she would do it alone—if she had to.

Her research began in earnest; obsessive, day and night. Within a week she had applied for and gained urgent leave. She was on her way to the largest exporting country of python skins in the world.

~

Working as a driver, Perdana earned his money by taking tourists to places of interest, stopping along the way to the shops of his 'cousins'. He owned a run-down, non-descript bucket of a car just like everyone else and relied on generous tips from tourists, especially those that had difficulty with the exchange rate.

'*Selamat pagi*, Madam. Welcome to Indonesia, home of the gods, paradise on earth. Madam, madam, you need driver, I give you good price, best price today, come on madam, I take you to hotel,' he rambled as he followed her out of the airport.

'I'm staying at the Mandala Bungalows, how much?' she asked.

'Normally, 20,000 rupiah but for you 19,000, best price today.'

'Fifteen thousand and you've got a deal,' she stated.

The next morning Perdana was waiting outside her apartment complex, smoking a cinnamon cigarette and laughing with the other drivers who were queued up waiting for tourists. The street smelt damp, rancid, dry and humid, with the occasional waft of pure, sweet frangipani flowers. The smells, sounds and rush of people made her feel quite heady and she would have spent the day acclimatising at the beach if the venom inside wasn't pulsating through her veins.

'Perdana, I would like to find someone who can

supply my company with snake-skins', she said, 'we want to make handbags, belts, watchbands and shoes.'

'Madame Arna, I will be taking you wherever you want to go,' he said, 'and I take you to some good shops too, my cousin do beautiful wood carvings.'

'Not today Perdana, I am here for work, I need to get down to business.'

'Ah, we will see madam Arna, we will see.'

'No, we will not see, I need to learn everything I can about the snake industry Perdana, that is what I'm here for.'

'Yes, madam Arna, please, please hop in, take a seat, we will go to see my other cousin.'

Along the way, out of town and into the countryside, they made idle chatter. The rice paddies were a picture, layered and sculptured in blocks of green. Farmers in hats tended them whilst children ran and played beside them. Offerings to the gods were placed upon everyone's doorstep, with flowers, fruit and burning incense. She began to feel more relaxed.

The car swerved to the side of the road and screeched to a halt.

'Madam Arna, look, the farmers are catching a snake, you want to see it?' he asked.

'Yes, yes, I want to see it!' she replied.

Three men with large sticks were chasing the snake through the wet slosh of a palm oil plantation. It was moving faster than you would imagine for a forty-six kilo, five-metre long python. Finally, they were on top of it. It raised its head and hissed. One of the men struck it across the head so hard that its head slapped back down hard against the ground. The thud was so hard that the snake was stunned. Arna gulped, but knew she had to swallow hard. The men hardly even noticed her, their only interest in the extra income this python would make their family this week.

One of the men quickly grabbed its head, while another got a stick that the snake wrapped itself around. It squeezed tightly enough to kill the perpetrator of that slap, but was hastily thrown into a white plastic bag, the stick pulled out and the bag tied tight. She could see it squirming and couldn't imagine how it could even breathe. As the farmers rushed away, Perdana started yelling at them in Indonesian. They came back and he handed them some cash in exchange for the snake—the equivalent of $10. When they reached the car he opened the boot and threw it in like an old piece of rubbish. The thud of its body against the rusted, metal boot made her cringe.

'What are you going to do with that snake, Perdana?' she asked.

'Sell it to my cousin Ular,' he said.

'Excellent,' she said, 'I'm coming.'

There were no formalities when they arrived at the skinnery. Although passively following Perdana, her eyes scrutinised every corner. She was shocked at how open they were to her, blazé and uncaring, nothing hidden as she had expected from this black market operation.

Perdana walked in and threw the bag on a heap in an open room. There were about one hundred similar bags, some writhing, some not. The whole time she had her handbag under her arm, the camera activated, hidden in the fake jewels along the edge.

'How long do you keep the snakes in the bag?' she asked a man sitting in the room, slurping rice noodles from his dish, splashing stains onto his t-shirt.

'It depend on the day, it depend on the week, …sometime one week, sometime two week, you need enough snake to do the skinning day…just depend,' he said and went on eating.

'You owe me for that snake,' Perdana reminded him.

'Yeah, yeah,' he replied and waved him along.

They walked out through to the back where skinny, emancipated looking dogs lazed around in the dirt. The men were going about their work in only shorts and the women wore t-shirts and cotton sarongs. There was a smell of foreboding in the air; foreboding mixed with sweat—both stale and fresh, cigarette smoke, the iron scent of fresh blood and rotten meat. Ular managed the business although you would never assume it by the casualness of his character and attire. His demeanour changed when Perdana introduced him to Arna and told him of her business interests. He quickly stood on his bare feet and smiled as he shook her hand and introduced himself.

'Here goes,' she thought. Her questions were as ready as her flirtatious smile:

'Can you supply my company with snake skins to make handbags and other fashion accessories?'

'Is $50 per metre the best price you can do for the highest quality, fully patterned skins?'

'Do you sell reticulated and red, blood python skins?'

'How many metres can you supply per month?'

'Do the skins come tanned?'

'Which fashion houses do you sell to in Europe?'

'Can we beat the system by not certifying all the skins in the trade?'

'Do you breed any pythons or just catch them all in the wild?'

He answered. He lied. She knew it. They got on well despite their hidden deceptions.

'You know Ular, I'm really interested to learn more about the snake trade. I would find it fascinating to see how you make the skins, would I be able to come and watch how it's done?' she smiled.

'Come next Tuesday, we do skinning day, wear old clothes, gets messy,' he replied.

She spent the next two days at the beach—her mind racing, overloaded. In the evenings she began editing the footage she had taken so far. Watching it over and over again was already strengthening her, each time her emotions were a little less raw. Her biggest challenge lay ahead—she knew that.

Perdana was waiting on Tuesday morning, smiling, happy to see her. Her heart was beating hard and her palms were sweaty. The drive seemed fast. They arrived before she felt ready. Handbag under her arm, she followed Perdana to the skinning room. There were two men untying the bags and shaking the listless, confused snakes out onto the floor. When they had released a pile of about twenty they started the killing. One man had a hammer, the other a metal pole and both were hitting them over the head. The fortunate ones died instantly, others fearfully tried to escape and were hit again, others just lay in the heap writhing in pain. There were four rounds of this heartless slaughtering.

~

One man went along and picked up each snake, passing it to the other, who hooked them onto thick metal hooks by their heads, some still alive writhing and hissing weakly. Dead or lingering near to it, they were then filled with water via a hose thrust roughly down their throats. They hung in the breeze like big, fat elongated balloons.

'This stretch the body and the skin,' a worker said to her, 'we leave them here now, go for lunch, come back in three hours.'

Perdana had busied himself cleaning up the bags and hosing down the bloodied concrete. He hadn't paid her much attention either. She requested to be taken back to her hotel complex and asked him to pick her up for the afternoon session. She needed to rest. The cruelty and brutality had drained her. She collapsed on the bed, releasing all the sorrow and hatred.

The process was quick. The snakes were decapitated and slit straight down the underside of their bellies. The skin then ripped off from top to tail. The gallbladder removed and collected in a bucket for a sideline business; dried and sold for traditional Chinese medicine. The flesh was thrown into a bucket to be minced and also sold on the side. The eggs found inside the females, thrown on the ground for the dogs to eat—sustaining the species, diminished in a gulp.

A quick wash of the skins in a dirty bucket of bloodied water and they were taken straight to the man who stretched them on a wooden board pinning the skins with nails.

Her fictitious 'negotiations' with Ular were done over the phone from that point onwards. She feigned illness as her excuse to not go back there. It gave her time to complete her editing and implement her next step.

Perdana reliably picked her up to take her to the airport. On the way, they had to swerve three times to avoid hitting rats.

'Sorry madam Arna, but we have a rat plague, it get worse every year. I should run them down but they make too much mess on the car,' he laughed.

~

It took her just four clicks:

- one copy to the international animal trade governing body,
- one copy to a list of world animal protection societies
- one copy to her editor, and

- one copy to her Facebook page.

Her story went viral, crazy viral, unexpectedly viral. Public support was overwhelmingly positive. The death threats were petrifying. She had daily interviews for newspapers, magazines and T.V. both in Australia and around the world.

Her editor at *Australian News*, although not impressed with her going behind his back, could not hide his happiness at increased sales and reader response. He called her into his office to run down how he planned to handle the whole situation. At the end, with a smirk on his face, he presented her with a small gift that would 'remind' her of this time in her career.

She opened the box and peered inside—stunned and speechless, she walked back to her desk. She didn't even turn off her computer. She picked up her handbag and walked out the door.

The Test

Erica Tippett

Will you look at us by the river![16] What a sorry sight. Me and Charlie. We sit forlornly on a cold, crumbling rock and stare into the rapidly flowing water. Contemplating, but not knowing, our fate. Deep thoughts, for so early in the morning…

~

Meg looked up, something had broken her concentration. She had been sitting on the rock for nearly an hour, completely still save for intermittent blinking. Her eyes darted around. Charlie raised an ear, then his furry head,

---

[16] First line from *Cloudstreet,* Tim Winton

cocked it to one side, then lowered it again with a quiet grunt. The river, oblivious, gurgled and splashed onwards. Meg returned her gaze to the river. Its crystal-clear waters were spring fed, bubbling up from deep underground. It had been attracting those in need of quiet reflection for longer than Meg could imagine. As she summoned the strength to leave, she wondered if her mother had ever sat on that same rock and peered into the cool water. She had so much to learn. At times, she felt like she knew nothing. Even with all the questions she had asked over the years, there were so many unanswered. She was sure she had barely scratched the surface. A single hot tear trickled down her cheek. She wiped it away and stared at the stones and leaves that lay on the riverbed. Meg took a deep breath in and stood. Charlie stood obediently by her side, and they left.

~

Meg checked the time. It was 6.30am. She busied herself in the kitchen. Once the correct formula had been entered in the food machine, she perched on a stool and waited for her breakfast. Meg ate slowly, carefully chewing each mouthful. She washed her food down with a glass of sanitised water. She set the dishbot to clean, then headed to the interior portal. She hesitated in the portal, relishing the warmth from the bright light above her head.

'You can do this,' Meg said under her breath, then pressed hard on the washroom button.

She used the sanitising cubicle, then dressed in the

clothes she had chosen the night before. After brushing her teeth, she glanced in the mirror and smiled. Meg had always had a lovely smile. Her inherited straight teeth had been a larger blessing than she had realised when a child, but that could be said for many of her attributes. It seemed cruel that Meg's good genetic standing could all be for nothing if she didn't perform well in a few hours. This was her last chance. She turned and left the washroom before the anxiety in her eyes was reflected back at her.

Meg grabbed her computer and hugged it tight to her chest before adding it to her pre-packed bag. After the debacle of last time, she was determined to be well organised and stay calm. She glanced at her device. The ticks on the screen confirmed all was going to plan. Meg scanned her bag, closed it, then swung it onto her back.

She shut the front door and locked it behind her using her thumbprint. She moved her hand, pressed it against the cold metal and closed her eyes. Her hand pulsed with the connection to her childhood home. She couldn't fathom not being able to return there.

'I will pass!' Meg said emphatically. She drew her hand back by her side, turned, and walked down the path.

Meg reached the station three minutes before the train. She looked to her device and received the smiling-faced confirmation her train was still on time. She sat on the cold metal seat, bag still on her back. A fellow passenger sat beside her. He was dressed in a navy pin-stripe suit, white shirt, no tie. Meg glanced sideways at the man, then rose from her seat and walked over to the shield glass to wait the remaining minute or so there. She hoped she would get a seat to herself on the train, which she had chosen to ensure a timely arrival and because it was not usually crowded.

As the train departed Meg looked out of the window from her seat and watched a woman in green slow from a run to a walk, then stop. The woman dropped her head, red-cheeked, breathing heavily. The woman looked defeated. Despite herself, Meg smiled wryly, then self-consciously uncurled her mouth and turned her attention back to her last-minute cramming. The words and diagrams swirled around in her head. Then she saw her mum's face. Oh, how she missed her on days like this. She felt like it could be the difference. If her mum was still around she would have started from the same base as most other girls and was sure she would have passed. Her therapist had disagreed.

'You feel like losing your mum at such a young age has put you on the backfoot. Stop looking for excuses, Meg. There are so many resources out there to help you. Don't dwell on the past. You can't change that. Just get on with it and pass the test.'

Meg had changed therapists. But that hadn't stopped those words being repeated in her dreams for months afterward.

Meg walked towards the foreboding entrance of Exam Centre #204 and through the double glass doors. After completing the obligatory fingerprinting and retina scan, she obtained her pass from the security booth and headed straight for the toilet. Meg sat there longer than necessary, muttering affirmations under her breath. At the sanitising station, she glanced sideways at the woman beside her. The woman had a round, unlined face. Meg watched the woman cleanse her hands and tidy her hair as if in any old facility. Then she looked down at her own hands, which had been cleansed a second time by accident. Meg kept her head low as she swung her bag on her back and quickly left the restroom.

When the doors opened to the exam hall, Meg filed in after the line of women in front. She had purposefully lingered in the hall until she could count eighteen in the queue, before casually walking over and joining the end. Meg sat at a pod on the far side of the vast room, in the front row of the second section. It was as far away as possible to where she had sat the first, and second time. She retrieved her water bottle from the side of her bag and sat down. Meg reached into her pocket and fingered the lucky charm her fiancé had given her over two years before. It hadn't worked, but somehow Meg couldn't suppress the impulse to bring it with her. She had left it in the top draw of her desk safely wrapped in a tiny garment. She was half-way through packing her bag when she saw it in her mind's eye and next thing she knew it was in her hand. Meg had sat on her bed turning it over with her fingers. And with each rotation, she had thought about a different incorrect answer from the past tests. But after a while, her mind wandered to the excitement on her fiancé's face when he had given her the lucky charm, the twinkle of hope in his eye. And it had felt lucky, again. So, Meg had shoved it in the pocket of the pants chosen for the big day. She shifted in her seat, pushed the charm back down to the bottom of her pocket and, blinking the memories away, picked up the skeletal helmet in front of her and put it on her head.

In what seemed like no time at all she heard the examiner call, 'times up,' his voice bouncing around the room.

Meg turned her head swiftly one way then the other, eyes panic-stricken. 'Remove your helmet, unhook your device blocker and leave it neatly at your pod. Then take your belongings and leave in an orderly manner.'

Meg did as she was told and anxiously filed out of the room in a reversed queue from the one hours before. Once safely out of the room, the group of women erupted into excited chatter.

'How do you think you went?' a rosy-cheeked girl asked Meg while they queued for the toilet.

'Ah, not sure. Okay, I think. Better than last…'

'Oh, you've taken the test before then?' the girl said.

Meg nodded, avoiding the girl's gaze by staring at her red shoes. 'How about you?'

'Really good, I think. I'm pretty sure. At least we don't have long to wait to find out the result. I still can't believe they take you into the clinic and perform the procedure straight away if you're in the top group. It's so exciting. I thought you would have to book it in for another day for sure.'

'Yeah, it is good,' Meg said and headed for a vacant cubicle. She sat on the toilet and waited until a few minutes after the red shoes had passed by the door on the way back to the sanitising station.

~

'Listening, please,' the authoritative voice broke through the chatter in Waiting Area B. 'All those whose names I call move quietly to room B1.'

Meg felt for the silver baby bottle charm in her pocket once more. Her fingers gripped the cool metal tightly and she clenched her other hand into a fist. She listened eagerly for her name, knowing the first group was the one she wanted to be in. They were the lucky ones, with no limits and immediate treatment. By the end of the day they would be fertile and free to choose how many children they had. There would be fifty in all.

The long list came to an end without her. Meg looked around the room and saw red shoes still sitting in the waiting room. The earlier shine in her eyes had vanished. Meg grinned, then slightly ashamed, dropped her eyes to the floor.

'Thank you for your patience, infertiles.' The announcement stirred the sullen room. 'Can those whose names I call move into room B2. If I do not call your name, please proceed immediately to the security desk and return your pass. If this was your first or second attempt you may reapply for next year's exam. If it was your final attempt your failure notice will be filed with the

Ministry of Population Management directly.'

Meg felt her chest tighten. She held her breath.

'Sal Jones.'

'Lou Ng.'

Red shoes sprang from her seat and rushed to the designated meeting room.

'Emi House.'

'Ana Navickaja.'

'Eva Garcia.'

As the names were called and each woman rose from her seat with a relieved smile, Meg felt more and more despondent.

'Wen Song.'

'Lee Ngo.'

'Peg Wiven.'

Meg's heart and stomach sank. Her mind raced. She was sure the multiple-choice answers she had selected had been correct. Most of them seemed familiar from the practice tests and only one or two had answers that seemed too alike to choose definitively. It was the cognitive process score she was worried about. She couldn't tell if the amount of time it took for the right answer to enter her head had been reasonable. And then there was the negative thought pattern component. That was what had brought Meg down before and resulted in the two failed attempts. She had tried her hardest to change her negative thought responses to positive. It had been excruciating trying to change her pessimistic reflex to optimistic. Meg had endured many hours of remedial training, which her father had begrudgingly paid for.

'Well, if it's the only way you will fulfil your purpose and bear me grandchildren,' he had said with a sigh.

It was alright for him, she had thought, he was exempt. Like all men, he had no real comprehension of what it was like to take the test. And fail. Her brother was just as bad, maybe worse.

'Don't worry about it, sis, if you never have kids then I'll get all the inheritance. I don't mind.'

Meg had looked at her brother's smug grin and wished her mum had been there to scold him.

~

Meg raised her head slowly from where it lay resting in her hands. She had an imprint from her engagement ring on her forehead. She looked at the solitaire diamond sparkling in the harsh neon light.

~

'Meg, will you do me the honour of being my wife?' Rus had asked her that warm summer night. The heady scent of jasmine had filled her nose and she had felt giddy with happiness and love. 'Take this ring, it was my mother's and my grandmother's before her. We have traced the ring back fifteen generations. And once you pass the test, we will be permitted to marry. Then one day the ring will pass to our daughter. That's what I will choose first when you ace the test. A baby girl.'

~

The room was half-empty. The tall, heavy-set figure at the

front looked to the last name on his list. He blinked twice.

'Megan Tinkard,' he said.

About the Authors

Bishnu Addison

Bishnu is a retired high school teacher. Her hobbies are writing, reading crime fiction and the classics. She's a self-confessed writing workshop 'junky' hunting for gems. She joined the Monash Writers Group when it was first established in 2013. The monthly meetings facilitated initially by David McLean, and then by Margaret Hepworth and Robert New, have fuelled her motivation and interest in writing. For Bishnu, a highlight of the meetings is when fellow writers share their writing which inspires the rest of the group. She wishes to thank Peter Head, Monash Council, and Wheelers Hill library staff for the venue and support.

Mube Akinci-Desem

Writing is Mube's passion. She writes poetry and is currently working on an historical fiction manuscript which she hopes to publish in the near future. Mube's daily walks feed her writing spirit. She is also learning Japanese and Greek.

The reason Mube chose the first line is to do with adaptation and evolution. 'Cockroaches have been around a lot longer than we have and consequently can comment on adapting to their environment.'

Sasha Buntman

Sasha Buntman is passionate about communicating, organising, digital marketing and independent publishing. Her purpose in life has always revolved around the art of organising. Organising the layout of elements on your page or in your book; organising words, sentences and messages together to create something meaningful and worthwhile for your audience.

As the founder of Midnight Media, Sasha provides affordable self-publishing solutions for fiction and non-fiction. Sasha project manages everything for you and ensures that your self-publishing journey runs smoothly and successfully.

Copywriting is another obsession of Sasha's. Her subsidiary business, Midnight Marketing, provides digital marketing support services to authors and entrepreneurs: including email, website and social media content management; copywriting; advertising and more.

Stephen Ellis

Stephen is based in Melbourne, Australia. He enjoys drawing, painting, movies, friendships, travelling, and writing children's adventure short stories. He chose the first line to play with the idea of time as a trope for this children's story.

Ingrid Fry

Ingrid is the author of the soon to be published Crystal Sphere series—a set of speculative fiction thrillers set in Australia—and two self-illustrated children's books. An astrologer who prepared her chart many years ago said, 'your destiny is to be either a nun, or a writer'. For Ingrid, the choice was a no-brainer, even though writing sometimes makes her feel as cloistered as a nun.

A writer, business development consultant, and minder of a husband and a beagle with super-powers, she lives in a leafy suburb on the outskirts of Melbourne. When she's not writing, you can find her pistol shooting at the local gun club, dancing her socks off at The Caravan Music Club, or being a passionate karateka, inching ever closer to a black belt in karate.

Sakuntala Gananathan

Sakuntala is a retired chartered accountant. Her historical novel White Flowers of Yesterday was published in the U.S. and was awarded Editor's Choice by her publishers, iUniverse.

An excerpt of their appraisal: 'The author has done a

fantastic job of weaving setting, characterisation, historical information, dialogue and plot together to create a complete, unique and compelling story...' while Kirkus Review wrote '...a surfeit of grace and wit...'

Sakuntala takes an active interest in the Tamil Senior Citizens Fellowship (Victoria) Inc, a non-profit association, of which she is the honorary treasurer for the current year. In 2013 her short story, 'Mend a Bend', earned her a prize at the Monash Word Fest Short Story Competition.

Margaret Hepworth

An author and educator, Margaret is a thought leader in peace education and founder of The Gandhi Experiment.

Margaret has been Head of Campus at Preshil School and holds a Master of Educational Studies. Her first novel, *Clarity in Time*, published in 2012, explores how the protagonist comes to understand that to make a difference in this world, you can no longer remain a passive bystander. Her most recent book, *The Gandhi Experiment: Teaching our teenagers how to become global citizens* has been endorsed by Rajmohan Gandhi, Gandhi's grandson. As the creator and author of Collaborative Debating, Margaret has developed a refreshing approach to non-adversarial, solution-focused debating into schools and the corporate world. Next stop, Parliament!

Her belief in what she is trying to achieve—to help

others step forward to make a difference in this world through passion and purpose—gives Margaret the drive and commitment required to help achieve more peace in this world through peace education.

'Fortitude' is the prologue to Margaret's novel, *Clarity in Time.* Permission was granted from the Nelson Mandela Foundation in South Africa to use Mandela as a fictional character.

Margaret is the recipient of the *2016 Sir John Monash Award for Inspirational Women's Leadership.*

Marlene Laurent

Born in Australia, Marlene grew up in the post-war suburb of South Oakleigh. Brought up a Catholic she entered the convent at the age of 17 after attending boarding school in Fremantle WA. She left the convent following the Ecumenical Council when changes were implemented in the Catholic Church.

She went on to train as a teacher and teaching became a passion. She was actively involved in in the Victorian education system and implemented many changes to the curriculum at her schools during her career.

On retiring, she decided to pursue her interest in writing, something she had always enjoyed doing.

Marlene lives in East Bentleigh and spends her time cycling, keeping fit at the local gym, reading, writing and travelling. She is member of the Australian Conservation Association, The Wilderness Society and other conservation groups. She takes an interest in her local community, as Secretary of the Glen Eira Residents Association.

Sung-Ju Suya Lee

Suya received a BFA from York University, Canada, an MBA from Bradford University School of Management, UK, and a PhD in Media & Communication from RMIT University, Australia. As part of her creative practice PhD, she wrote a farce comedy screenplay, which was long-listed for the ScreenCraft Comedy screenplay contest. One of her short stories was short-listed for the inaugural Apollo Writers Festival short story contest.

Besides being a student and travelling, she has had many 'day' jobs to support her writing, filmmaking and acting career. She feels privileged to be a part of The Monash Writers Group.

Bala Mudaly

Bala is a psychologist and retired only this year at the age of 80. Oakleigh has been his home for the past 29 years, since he migrated from South Africa with his wife. Bala is partial to writing essays and short stories, which are usually set in Oakleigh and surrounding suburbs. He took up writing as a hobby two years ago when he noticed a slow decline in his spelling and creative writing skills. He is particularly fascinated with how characters in fiction come into being, take on a persona of their own, and often outlive their creator.

Robert New

Robert has degrees in Psychology, Sociology, Biology and Education, which he uses in his writing. He is a Psychology and Science teacher and also an author and publisher. His novel, *Incite Insight*, has been described as "smart and imaginative" and "deceptively educational of the human condition."

Sever-Reign, one of the short stories in his collection *Movemind* was 'Highly Commended' in the Monash Wordfest (2017) competition and he's been a winner and runner-up of the RAS short story competition. Robert is the author of *The Conversationist*, *Incite Insight*, *MoveMind, Mug Punter* and the forthcoming *Colours of Death: Sgt Thomas' Casebook*. Robert is mildly kosmemophobic.

Andy Russell

Two years ago Andy retired as an electronics engineer. At school English was one of his least favourite subjects. Now, after years of technical writing, it does not seem so difficult after all. As one of his retirement activities, he is enjoying writing fiction.

Robert Sayegh

Robert has always been fascinated by … things, from science and engineering to design, philosophy and people's relations in general.

Married with two kids and a secret identity as a software engineer and manager, in bursts of spare time

Robert focuses on writing, both in Arabic and English. Robert is currently working on his first draft for children's chapter book and hopes to publish it in 2018. He is also putting together a collection of poems in English to publish in 2019, under the title *Reflections; mind and heart discussing relationship*. The short story included in this anthology is inspired by real people close to him.

Brook Tayla

Brook has a Diploma of Teaching (Primary) and a Graduate Diploma in Children's Literature. She currently works part-time as a librarian and runs her own children's literature review blog called 'Tell Tales To Me'.

As a member of many writers' groups, prominent literary related associations, and reviewer for online children's magazines, blogs and publishers, Brook has extensive experience and expertise in her chosen field. This year she is honoured to have the role as a CBCA (Children's Book Council of Australia) judge for the 2019 Book of the Year - Eve Pownall Award.

Brook likes to write stories for children but also enjoys the allusiveness of short story writing. She has previously had a short story published in the *Short and Twisted* anthology (2017) and also enjoys entering literary competitions.

Apart from being a writer, Brook is also an animal activist and her factional story is based on an aspect of animal cruelty in the fashion industry.

Erica Tippet

Erica's love of story was developed as a child and she has fond memories of her dad reading bedtime stories every night. An aspiring writer, she was reminded by the passing of her dad that life is too short to just talk about the things you want to do; and has now written a book that she hopes to publish soon. Erica has always had a keen interest in all things international and hopes to promote diversity of voice and perspectives through an upcoming writing project. Her short story 'The Test' is the first story she has had published since her school days. Erica chose her first line from a book by one of her favourite Australian authors. She remembers reading *Cloudstreet* as a teenager, and it had a profound impact on her. She loves descriptive writing that gives the reader a true sense of place, and transports them somewhere new.

This collection of short stories was written by the members of the Monash Writers Group, based around the theme of 'the view from the hill'.

Each writer has interpreted the theme in a unique way and the collection includes stories from a variety of genres.

ISBN: 978-0-9944399-5-6

Available to order from bookshops and online retailers including Amazon.com.
http://a.co/hIx6TBS

www.ingramcontent.com/pod-product-compliance
Ingram Content Group UK Ltd.
Pitfield, Milton Keynes, MK11 3LW, UK
UKHW040008200726
13854UKWH00001B/96

9 780648 327332